Chapter One

There were tiny lights glinting on the snow, as if the last breath of magic in the world had collected right outside the window. Luciana pressed her forehead against the cold glass and watched them form shimmering lines in the night-dark of the orchard, spinning apart every few minutes before coming together to dance again somewhere else. She knew it wasn't really magic. It would be Charley tramping about in the pasture between their two houses, hunting winter rabbits by the light of his portable gas lamp.

Luciana shut her eyes, wishing that she could turn back the clock. She already knew exactly when and where she would go. It would be to a time and place she held close in her heart and thought about often: the theatre, the one and only time she had seen the Golden Butterfly. In her mind she heard the orchestra start up, and suddenly Luciana was there again, watching from her seat. The lights on the stage were full and bright. The theatre was packed to the rafters and the air fizzed with excitement. Everyone there knew that they were about to witness something spectacular: the most extraordinary illusion ever performed. Then her grandfather stepped into the spotlight and the audience erupted with rapturous applause. They were all under the spell of the Magnificent Marko, and they wanted to see the wonder that he had promised them. They wanted to see him transform a woman into a butterfly.

Luciana's grandfather raised his wand and his assistant appeared from the other side of the stage in a dress of shimmering gold silk. The audience fell into silence. The Magnificent Marko waved his wand through the air and drew her out of the shadows, into the light cascading from above. Tiny jewels glinted in her hair, her dress flowed around her like water. She was magic personified, wonder sewn into her every movement. She reached the centre of the stage and the Magnificent Marko flicked his wand. She began to rise into the air, as lightly as a mote of dust. A susurration ran around the auditorium: the sound

The Golden Butterfly

Sharon Gosling

Stripes

of five hundred people all drawing in their breath. Then wings sprouted from the woman's back, gossamer-thin and stitched from the colours of moonlight.

The Golden Butterfly danced in the air, beautiful and impossible, yet there before their eyes. The audience murmured and laughed, astonished and delighted. Then the Magnificent Marko flicked his wand again. There was a shower of sparks, a bang and…

The Golden Butterfly vanished.

Luciana opened her eyes. Her forehead was still pressed against the cold window, and outside Charley's light was still bobbing on the snow. Her heart felt heavier than ever. There was no magic here. There was no magic anywhere. Not any more.

The murmuring in the shadows behind her grew a little louder. She recognized the whispers as first her grandfather's voice, then her grandmother's. Then, finally, there was Doctor Stott's.

"Luciana," her grandmother called quietly. "Your grandfather wants to talk to you, darling."

Luciana slid from the window ledge, landing lightly on the Persian rug. When she had been little, she had played in this room for hours. Her grandparents' four-poster bed had been her chariot then: in her mind it had been given wings to go with its lion's-paw feet. On it she

3

had ridden to faraway places, searching for the butterflies he had taught her about.

What did you find today, little chick?

Today I found the Distant's silverstreak, Grandfather.

And what would it be called in my books?

The Iraota distanti, *Grandfather.*

Wonderful! And where did you find it?

In a place called Sumatra.

Very good, little chick, very good. Now show me Sumatra on the globe, and draw me a picture of the butterfly's wings, and then I will show you how to make a coin appear from Charley's right ear.

She stepped into the puddle of candlelight around the bed. Her grandfather was small among the shadows, propped up by white pillows. Luciana was dismayed by how frail he looked. She reached out and took his hand. "I'm here, Grandfather. I have been here all the time."

Her grandfather smiled. "I know you have, my dear. What a good child you have been for us."

His voice was hoarse and thin, like the winter wind. Where was the giant who had often carried her on his shoulders? Where was the man she had once seen turn a woman into a butterfly in front of a theatre full of people? The patient teller of funny stories who had finally managed to banish her nightmare fear of fire? Luciana felt

4

tears pricking her eyes.

"Now, now," her grandfather said gently. "There is no need for that. I have had a good life, a very full life. Everything changes, Luciana, but that does not mean that everything ends, even when it seems to. Remember the caterpillar and its cocoon; the butterfly it becomes. There are wonderful things ahead of you. I want you to try to be happy, my dear."

Luciana felt the tears weighing on her eyelashes. In that moment she could not imagine ever feeling happy again. Then Doctor Stott asked her to move away. Luciana squeezed the frail fingers in hers once more and let them go. She went back to her place on the windowsill. Outside, Charley's light had disappeared. Instead she watched through her own reflection as the night turned into a new day. By the time the stars were lost to the low sun of winter, her grandfather had faded with them.

*

"Do you remember," Charley asked, "the time that your grandpa pulled a whole string of silk scarves out of half a walnut shell?"

It was a week later, a Tuesday, and the day of Marko Cattaneo's funeral. Charley had tramped up the hill from the vicarage, where his mother was housekeeper. He'd been doing that since he was old enough to walk, and before that his mother had brought him in her arms. Over the past week he and Luciana had wandered the house together, five storeys that held memories of their shared childhoods. Luciana was struggling to comprehend that Marko would never be there again. She had been an orphan since she was two and she couldn't remember her parents at all, however hard she tried. Her grandparents were her whole family – apart from Charley, who might as well have been a brother – and now, at thirteen, with Marko gone, Luciana felt as if she had lost half the landscape of her world.

Charley's words prompted a memory: the two of them kneeling right there on the rug in the drawing room, her grandfather sitting in his favourite chair. It was a rainy day and Marko had been keeping them entertained. The room had been chilly, but they had not lit the fire. That was back when Luciana's dreams had been so haunted by flames that she could not bear to be near one, even in daylight. Charley had brought them a blanket each and they had watched as Marko pulled the shell from his pocket. He held it up for Luciana and Charley to inspect before turning it over and tapping it with one finger, as if shaking out a bug trapped in a glass. A corner of bright blue silk had poked from the shell. Her grandfather had tugged at it and a whole line of silk scarves had appeared, sheet after sheet of vivid colour pulled into existence from nowhere.

Luciana laughed. "That was so funny," she said. "You couldn't believe it!"

"Neither could you," her friend said, grinning. "I think I'm still deaf from you shrieking in my ear."

Luciana thumped him lightly on the arm. "Yeah, but I'm the one who learned how to do it for myself."

"You did not," Charley scoffed.

"I did!"

"I don't believe you," the boy said, and then sighed. "I don't believe anyone could do magic like that except the Magnificent Marko."

The use of her grandfather's stage name brought a new lump to Luciana's throat. She looked up at the old framed poster on the wall. It had been colourful once – daubs of yellows, reds, greens and blues – but now the bright hues were beginning to fade.

The Magnificent Marko!
Be Amazed!
Be Intrigued!
Be Flabbergasted!
See the Greatest Magician Alive!

He had performed at a big theatre in London three

7

nights a week and Luciana and her grandmother would attend a show once each month. Sometimes, as a treat, Charley would go with them. What excitement those days would always bring! The bumpy carriage ride to the station, then the train journey from the country into the smoky city. It felt like magic itself to watch the landscape transform as they steamed closer to the metropolis. The fields grew smaller, turning first into gardens and then into mazes of streets. The colours would change too, from vivid watercolour-greens into drab angles of grey and brown, brick-red and ochre.

Then just before Luciana's ninth birthday and at the height of his fame, the Magnificent Marko had vanished from the stage himself. No one had ever told Luciana why her grandfather had stopped performing, and every time she had asked, he had simply smiled. *Not everything is meant to last forever, little chick,* he would say. *Now, show me how to chase the king of clubs. I know you have watched me do it.* Overnight her grandfather had ceased to practise his talents, abandoning the world of magic without explanation. Luciana missed it, and knew that her grandfather did too. She'd often found him reading *The Magician's Times* and sighing mournfully. But he would never tell her why.

Now, four years later, the Magnificent Marko was gone for good.

Luciana went to the small table beside the fire. Pulling open its little drawer she took out the empty walnut shell. With one hand she held it up for Charley to see, quickly using her other hand to fold the thin sheaf of silk, which had been in the drawer beneath it, into her sleeve before he noticed.

"Here," Charley said, astonished. "That's not the same one, is it?"

Luciana held up the shell and tapped it, just the way her grandfather had. A glimpse of purple silk pushed its way out of the shell. She pulled at it and there was another colour behind it, blue this time, then red, then green, then yellow. Charley stared as the scarves floated down to settle on the floor around their feet.

"I told you," she said, laughing again, happy that she hadn't forgotten how to perform the trick.

"But how—" Charley began, when he'd found his voice.

He was interrupted by the door opening. Luciana's grandmother, face pale and back stiff in her black mourning dress and veil, gave a small smile.

"It is time, my dears," she said. "The carriage is here to take us to the church. Are you ready?"

Luciana nodded. She didn't put the shell back in the

drawer. She slipped it into the sleeve of her dress instead, and gathered up the silks too. It seemed important to have something of her grandfather with her as they said a final goodbye.

Chapter Two

The snow began to fall again as the mourners stood by Marko's graveside. Luciana lifted her face and let the flakes land on her cold cheeks and the curls that had escaped from beneath her black bonnet. Charley slipped his hand into hers and she squeezed his fingers. When it came time for her to scatter a handful of earth on her grandfather's coffin, she let go of the walnut shell too. With it went the bright silks. The scarves drifted down to cover his last resting place. Marko would have loved the flash of vibrancy. His life had been full of colour. Why should his death be any different?

The other mourners began to filter away, but Luciana

and Charley remained at the graveside, even though Luciana's toes were becoming blocks of ice in her best black shoes.

"Come now," said her grandmother, slipping an arm round Luciana's shoulders and pulling her close. "We should go home, before we both catch a chill. Your grandfather wouldn't want that, would he? Charley, take your mother home, dear. We will see you tomorrow, I'm sure."

As Luciana turned away from Marko's grave, she remembered some of the last words he had said to her. *Everything changes, but that does not mean that everything ends.* But this, here, now, was an ending, as sure as there ever could be one.

*

They turned into their gate to find a large black carriage waiting beside their steps. Luciana's grandmother frowned as the hooves of their old grey mare crunched to a halt on the gravel behind it.

"Grandmother?" Luciana said, leaning forward to look out of the window. "Who is it?"

Before her grandmother could answer, both doors of the carriage opened and six men dressed in black suits and heavy black coats stepped out. One of these figures turned in their direction and Luciana felt her grandmother start in surprise. Then a look of intense dislike flashed across her pale face. Luciana was astonished. She could not remember her grandmother ever disliking anyone.

The man strode towards them. He was big, with dark eyes in a round, pale face. He reached the trap and looked up at them. Luciana felt a chill pass down her spine and coil itself in her gut.

"Isabella," he said in greeting. His voice was crushed glass, its edges sharp and unpleasant.

"Thursby," replied Luciana's grandmother. "What are you doing here? If you came to pay your respects, you are too late."

The man's lip curled. He held out a hand. "Please," he said. "Do let us try to make this as civil as possible."

Luciana watched as her grandmother hesitated for a second, then reluctantly allowed him to help her to the ground. Luciana followed but the man barely cast her a glance.

"You know why I'm here," Thursby said, once they both stood facing him.

"Oh yes, I know," said Luciana's grandmother calmly. "What you are looking for no longer exists, Thursby. And you are not welcome in this house."

He smiled coldly. "Welcome or not, Isabella," he said. "We will come in. For all his many – *many* – faults, Marko

13

at least understood the way of such things. And I do not believe that you can do without the widow's pension he arranged for you through the Society. Or perhaps you can. Shall we find out?"

Luciana stood watching, willing her grandmother to send this person away. But after a moment Isabella Cattaneo took a single step back.

"Go," she said, raising her chin stiffly towards the house. "But you will find nothing. Marko gave away or destroyed everything when you forced him from the stage."

"We shall see, dear lady." Thursby was already half turned towards the house. "After all, it would take a man – a magician – to recognize it."

Luciana watched as Thursby's bulk disappeared through their door. A shadow passed the drawing-room window: one of his men inside, searching for ... what?

Luciana reached out and touched her grandmother's hand. Isabella's fingers twitched, then grasped Luciana's tightly.

"Who are they?" Luciana asked.

Her grandmother shook her head, thin-lipped, and her grey eyes glinted with anger. "Men unworthy of our time or energy. Come, let us walk a little."

Luciana did not want to walk. She wanted to go into her house and throw out the men who were violating it,

14

but fear held her back. She allowed her grandmother's grip on her hand to remain as she was tugged towards the skeleton of their orchard.

"What did you mean," she asked, as they tramped through the snow, "when you said that Thursby had forced Grandfather from the stage?"

Her grandmother looked down at her, pale face highlighted by two flashes of pink anger tinting her cheeks. "It is not worth talking about, my dear," she said. "It is done with, it is gone. As Thursby and his men will be soon enough. Then that will be an end to it, once and for all. Marko is dead, and at least he will not be here to see the age of great magic fizzle out thanks to that *monster.*"

The vehemence in her grandmother's words shocked Luciana into silence.

When they returned to the house, the strange men were preparing to leave. A look of thunder was rolling around Thursby's face. Luciana felt the fear coiling in her stomach again, that horrible twist of dread.

"I told you it was not here," said Isabella Cattaneo, as he stalked down the steps. He moved past her without a word and she called after him, her strong voice rising with the wind. "This is the last time you will gain access to this house, Thursby. I am not bound by the rules that Marko swore to. Should you ever again set foot on my property,

I will call the constables. Marko is gone, and with him the Golden Butterfly. Let it *rest*."

Thursby paused but didn't turn back. A moment later he had vanished into the carriage. Then it clattered quickly out of their gate and away.

Luciana's grandmother did not watch them go. Instead she pulled her granddaughter into the house, both of them shivering. Luciana could feel the tread of those horrible men everywhere, as if they were still lurking in the shadows of their home.

"Go into the drawing room," said her grandmother. "I will find you a change of clothes."

"Don't light the fire," Luciana heard herself say, as if from very far away. "Please don't light the fire."

Isabella stared at her. "But you haven't been afraid of the fire for a long time, my darling," she said. "A fire in a grate is safe, don't you remember? And anything else is nothing but a bad dream."

Still Luciana hesitated. The cold was eating into her bones, but the thought of sitting in front of a fire seemed at that moment to be the most terrifying thing in the world. It was daylight, but she felt herself surrounded by the same nightmare that had haunted her when she was little. It had been brought back by Thursby and his horrible men.

Her grandmother squeezed her shoulder gently. "Go,"

she said softly. "I will bring you a blanket instead."

Luciana did as she was told, her teeth beginning to chatter with cold and some other emotion she could not identify. She pushed open the door to the drawing room, walked inside, and stopped dead.

The poster of the Magnificent Marko was no longer on the wall. It lay on the floor, its frame smashed open and the poster itself torn in two.

Chapter Three

That night Luciana woke screaming, drenched in sweat and shaking with fear. Her grandmother was already there at her side, trying to soothe her.

"Hush," Isabella whispered. "You're safe now. Hush now, hush."

Luciana threw her arms round her grandmother's neck and Isabella hugged her close. Neither of them said anything for a few minutes.

"Was it the dream?" her grandmother asked eventually.

Luciana nodded. "The house was burning and I couldn't get out. There were flames everywhere, coming closer, and there was a man in the flames, all burnt, burning, and I—"

"Shh," said her grandmother, stroking her hair. "It's all

right. It was a nightmare, Luciana. It wasn't real."

"Why has it come back?" Luciana asked, her voice muffled against her grandmother's shoulder.

Isabella held her tighter. "I don't know, my darling. But we beat it before, didn't we? We can beat it again."

They huddled together under the coverlet until the light of a new day chased away the darkness of night.

*

"But who were they?" Charley asked the next day, when Luciana told him what had happened with Thursby and his men. "What did they want?"

They were sitting on the floor in the drawing room with blankets round their shoulders to ward off the cold. Luciana had told Charley about the return of her nightmare and how her awful fear of fire seemed to have come back. Charley had given her a hug and said that blankets were fine with him. Now they were playing with a deck of cards as they talked. Luciana had fanned them into a perfect semicircle face down on the rug between them.

"Grandmother thought it was the Golden Butterfly," she said. "Now, pick a card. Look at it, but be sure not to let me see it."

Charley took a card and glanced at it, but Luciana could tell he wasn't really concentrating as she collected the rest of the deck with one hand.

"Wasn't the Golden Butterfly the trick you got me into trouble with?"

Luciana bit her lip, feeling guilty but also fighting the urge not to laugh. "Um…"

"It was, wasn't it?" Charley exclaimed. "You wanted to do it yourself so you made me help you. Didn't we use one of your grandma's dresses and a rope from the stable?"

Luciana couldn't help it – she laughed. "Yes. I was convinced I had worked out how it was done and wanted to perform it in the hallway."

"That's right!" Charley shook his head as he remembered. "You made me hold you up on the rope while you dangled over the banister. Your grandma lost her rag when she saw what we were doing – and *I* got the blame for it! Everyone assumed it had been my idea. My mum was so upset – she thought I was going to be banished from the Big House forever!"

Luciana shook her head. "I used to get you into trouble like that all the time, didn't I? I'm so sorry. I just wanted to be the Golden Butterfly. It was so amazing – the most beautiful thing I've ever seen, even though I only saw it once."

"And your grandma thinks that's what this man Thursby was looking for?" Charley asked. "The Golden Butterfly? How can they have been looking for a trick?"

20

"I don't know." Luciana sighed, cutting the cards and holding out one half of the stack. "It doesn't make any sense to me either but Grandmother won't talk about it." Charley added his card to the pile in her hand and Luciana shuffled both together again.

"Have you checked to see that they didn't take anything away with them?" he asked.

"Everything seems to be in its rightful place," Luciana said, as she shuffled the deck. "Apart from the poster, that is."

Charley looked over at the two ragged halves of the colourful paper sheet. Luciana had gathered them up and put them on the table beside the empty fireplace. Ruined though it was, she couldn't bear to throw the poster away. The pieces were curling in on themselves, the torn paper dry and fragile.

"Why would they bother taking it off the wall?" Charley wondered. "Did they think there was something behind it? A safe?"

"Maybe," Luciana agreed. "But that doesn't explain why they tore it in half. There couldn't have been anything behind it, the frame is too thin." She fanned the deck again and slid out one card, face down. "Turn it over. Is that your card?"

Charley held up the queen of diamonds. "Yes, it is! How did you do that?"

"Magic, of course," she said with a quick grin, though the rush of happiness she'd usually feel from getting a trick right was absent.

"It's the other thing that Grandmother said that I keep thinking about," she told Charley. "She said that Thursby forced Marko from the stage. She obviously hated the man – I could see it in her face – and I've never known her to hate anyone."

They were both quiet for a while. Charley picked up the deck of cards and shuffled them. Watching him reminded Luciana of seeing her grandfather turning cards in his hands as he produced trick after astonishing trick. His manner was so quick, so smooth, so clever. Luciana had spent hours just watching him, trying to work out how he did it.

She got to her feet and went over to the two torn pieces of the poster. Picking them up, Luciana turned them over to look at the back.

"What are you looking for?" Charley asked, watching.

"I was just thinking," she said slowly. "You're right – you can't look for a trick, that doesn't make sense. But what if they're looking for the key to how the trick was done?"

Charley got to his feet. "You mean – the method? How it was constructed?"

Luciana nodded. "If so, they were probably looking for

something written down, weren't they? In a notebook, or on a piece of paper – that would make sense, wouldn't it? That would explain why they took the poster off the wall. Perhaps they thought it could be written on the back."

Charley looked down at the blank, yellowing back of the poster she held. "But it wasn't."

"So where else could it be?" Luciana bit her lip. "They went through all the papers in his desk – they left them in a mess. All the books in the library too."

"If there was something about this trick that was so important that he was forced off the stage because of it, Marko would have hidden it really well, wouldn't he?" Charley said. "Where would that be?"

"I don't know."

"Come on, Ana," Charley said. No one but him called her that – it had started when they were small and 'Luciana' was too difficult to say. Even now they were older, the name had stuck. "Think. I know you. Your mind works just like Marko's. It's in there, somewhere. *Think*."

Her eyes filled with tears and she looked away.

"I'm sorry," Charley said. "I didn't mean to upset you. It doesn't matter anyway. None of it matters. Like Mrs Cattaneo said, it is done with."

Luciana took a deep breath and dashed away the tears. "It does matter," she said. "It matters to me. Magic was my

23

grandfather's whole life, and now he's gone and I miss him *so* much. If there's a chance that some of his magic is still out there … I want to be the one to find it, not that horrible man or anyone else like him. Who is Thursby anyway, and how did he make my grandfather give up what he loved? And why he is looking for the Golden Butterfly now that Grandfather is dead? That was the Magnificent Marko's greatest trick. If the key to it is still out there somewhere, I can't let anyone else steal it!"

"OK," said Charley with a smile. "Then where do we start?"

Luciana looked down at the poster. Even as damaged as it now was, she loved to look at it. There was her grandfather, painted wearing his black magician's cloak and top hat, holding his magic wand.

"Thursby's men looked everywhere," she said, thinking aloud. "But they couldn't find what they were looking for."

"Maybe it's not here in your house at all, like your grandmother said?"

"Maybe…" Luciana stared at the image of her grandfather with his wand raised. *A magician's wand is his simplest but most important trick,* he had told her once. *It's all about misdirection. Distract people with the wand and they'll miss everything else, even if it's happening right in front of them.* "Or maybe they were just looking in the wrong place."

"Well then," Charley said. "Where would have been the right place?"

An idea was beginning to bloom in Luciana's mind. "They thought they were looking for something that was written down. That was my first thought too. But perhaps we should be looking for something else."

"Like what?"

Luciana stared at him, suddenly completely certain that she knew exactly where Thursby and his men should have been searching.

"Like a puzzle," she said, heading for the door with a confused Charley starting after her.

Chapter Four

Luciana pushed open the door into her grandfather's study. The walls were lined with many books, but the most striking object in the room was Marko's huge desk.

"I thought you said they went through all his papers and books?" Charley asked doubtfully, as Luciana went to it.

"They did," said Luciana.

Charley shrugged. "Then what are we doing here?"

"Isn't the desk amazing?" Luciana asked. "Just look at it!"

It was a huge piece of furniture. The large writing level was surrounded on three sides by shelves, cabinets and drawers that formed a cubicle tall enough to loom over them both. The whole was formed of many different types of wood, from the darkest ebony through the rosiest chestnut to the palest pine. There were so many tiny cupboards and sliding panels that it was impossible to count them all in just one glance, and each of these – as well as the rear panels behind the shelves – were all richly decorated. Some were inlaid with intricate geometric patterns, others had pictures of trees, flowers, landscapes or seascapes. The impression was of a detailed patchwork quilt made of wood. The more one looked, the more there was to see.

"Grandfather had it made for him," Luciana told Charley. "It took the carpenter years to make. When I was little I used to spend hours just opening and shutting all the drawers and doors."

She kneeled on the floor and pulled open the door of one of the two larger cupboards that stood either side of her grandfather's chair. Inside were concealed three more small drawers, all fitted with keyholes. The locks of each had been smashed open, the beautiful wooden patterns disrupted by jagged cracks and gaping holes. Luciana and Charley took in the damage in dismay.

"Well," Charley said, after a moment. "If whatever it was they were looking for was in one of those drawers, they would have found it."

Luciana looked up at him with a quick smile and then

moved around the side of the desk. The outer panels were just as elaborately decorated, though with a more abstract design. The background pattern was formed of uneven wavy lines, each constructed from small sections of different woods in varying shades. Within these were concentric circles, like the expanding ripples left after a stone is dropped into a pool of water, and scattered inside and between the waves and circles were small raised spurs of wood. The spurs looked as if they might be rivets that the carpenter had used to hold the desk together, but they were too randomly placed for that, dotted through the flow of wood like stones on a riverbed, some in clusters, others more spread out.

"That," Charley said, dropping to sit cross-legged beside Luciana, "is enough to make you dizzy just by looking at it."

Luciana smiled. "I used to stare at it for hours. I've always thought it looks like the stream down at the bottom of the orchard. I once heard Grandfather teasing Grandmother that he was testing a new type of hypnosis that kept small children quiet for hours. And then—"

She reached out, resting her fingers on one of the spurs. Then she used her thumb and forefinger to twist it. It turned, silently.

"It moves!" Charley exclaimed.

Luciana said nothing. Instead she turned another spur below the one she had first turned, then the one directly to the right, before moving to rotate the one to the right of the first she had moved. Once she had done so, there was a faint clicking sound. She and Charley watched as the circles within the invisible square she had created shifted a little with each click. As they did so, some of the connected pieces in the background flow of the 'river' shifted too, curving a different way, as if some of the water had got caught in a little whirlpool. A few of the wavy lines now formed new outlines around some of the little spurs of wood.

"It's a puzzle," Luciana explained. "I discovered it by accident when I was small. It's only this small section of the desk."

Charley looked dumbstruck. "What happens when you solve the puzzle? What does it look like when you have?"

"I don't know," Luciana said. "I've never completed it. It's the only time my grandfather told me not to do something. He saw me playing with the turning pieces and he said, 'My darling girl, you can have anything of mine you desire, but that is my secret and must remain so.' He asked me never to play with that part of the desk again, and so I never did. Actually, that was when he started teaching me how to handle the cards. He said a mind as sharp as mine had to be occupied in the best way possible. I was so excited that he was showing me magic that I forgot about the hidden puzzle completely. Until now. Because this," she said, indicating the rest of the ornate decoration on the desk, "this is all just misdirection, isn't it? The rest of the desk – all those patterns and pictures on the front – is a waving wand, distracting people so they don't see what's hiding right in front of them."

They both looked again at the pieces Luciana had rotated.

"Well," said Charley, sounding a little breathless, "I suppose now is the time to find out ... don't you think?"

Luciana nodded. She worked her way through all the spurs, making sure she turned all the ones that moved, until every circle and piece of the pattern behind it that could move had shifted. She had no idea what would happen once the final section had turned.

The answer was: not a thing.

She and Charley sat back and waited, but beyond subtle shifts in the pattern, nothing had really changed. Some of the circles and spurs were closer together, and more of the wavy lines in the background were connected up, but it still looked as haphazard as before she'd started.

"That can't be it, can it?" Charley said. "There must be something else to it."

"There must be another part of the puzzle that needs

completing," said Luciana. "Or maybe the lines aren't joining up in the right way."

"But how do you know what the right way is?" Charley asked. "How can you possibly know what it's supposed to look like to be correct?"

Luciana shook her head. "I don't know..."

She reached out again, running her fingers over the pieces of wood that had moved. They were uneven now. She pressed one here and there, wondering if there was some sort of release that had to be activated, but although several of the spurs did push in with a click, still nothing happened.

She sat back, frustrated. "I was so sure this was where my grandfather had hidden whatever Thursby was looking for."

Charley sighed. "It was a good thought. But maybe this is all there ever was to it. Another little sleight of hand."

"But then why wouldn't he let me play with it?" Luciana asked.

She remembered the surprised look on her grandfather's face, how quickly he had moved to stop her. *I'd better find something else to occupy you, hadn't I?* he'd said, smiling. *Come to think of it, it's high time you had your own deck of cards.*

Luciana frowned at the irregular shapes in front of her. There was something niggling at the back of her mind, but she just couldn't work out what it was.

"Come on," Charley said, after she'd stared at the desk for another ten minutes. "Why don't we go and ask if we can have some lunch? Mum sent an apple cake."

Luciana sighed. "All right," she said, and let him pull her to her feet. Disappointment bit like sickness in the pit of her belly as she followed Charley to the door. Then more of her grandfather's words echoed in her head.

Everything changes, but that does not mean that everything ends. Remember the caterpillar and its cocoon, the butterfly it becomes.

Luciana stopped. She looked back at the desk. "Wait," she called to Charley. "*Wait!*"

She dropped back to her knees in front of the panel. Charley was at her side in an instant.

"What is it?" he asked. "What have you seen?"

Luciana waved her hands at the whole side of the desk. "What does that look like to you?" she asked.

Charley blew out his cheeks. "I think you're right," he said. "If it looks like anything, it looks like a riverbed."

"No," Luciana said, "I'm wrong. It's not water, or pebbles, or anything like that."

Charley blinked. "What is it then?"

"It's butterflies," she said, almost laughing with the certainty of it all. "Don't you remember how Grandfather always loved them? We'd spend hours looking at his books

32

about butterflies. The spurs aren't stones, they're *dots*, and they *are* in patterns – they're the patterns on the wings of butterflies. Look, that cluster there – that looks like a Painted Lady. There's a Red Admiral, and that's one of the Fritillaries – I'd have to check which – and that's a little Speckled Wood. And that," she said, pointing to the section she had moved. "What does that look like to you now that it's in the right formation?"

Charley frowned, squinting his eyes and turning his head sideways.

"I'm not sure," he said. "Except that part of it almost looks like … an eye?"

"Yes, it does," she said. "Except it's not a real eye. It's a false one. Like you'd find on the wing of a male *Aglais io*."

"A what?" Charley asked.

"A peacock butterfly." Luciana traced between the circles with a fingertip, drawing a shape among what she had once thought was mere chaos. The spurs she had turned had begun to connect, but two were still not aligned. Now that she knew what she was looking for though, Luciana knew exactly how to correct it. She turned two of the spurs in the opposite direction to the others, and as she did so the wavy lines moved into place. There, as clear as day to her now, was the delicate outline of a wing, patterned exactly like a peacock butterfly. Her finger landed on the final spur and

Luciana felt it give under the pressure. She pressed it, hard. It clicked back into the wood. She repeated the journey around the newly formed wing shape, and as Luciana pushed in the final spur there was a loud *click*.

Chapter Five

Luciana slipped her fingers into the sliver of darkness that had appeared behind the butterfly's wing and pulled. A narrow drawer slid out. It had been made to fit in the space at the rear of the desk, behind the cupboard that hid the locked drawers smashed open by Thursby's men.

Inside there was a small pouch made of worn black velvet. Luciana took it out, loosened the cord holding it closed and emptied the contents into her palm.

"What on earth is that?" asked Charley.

Luciana had no idea. She held a slim, triangular piece of metal about the size of her palm, shaped like a half-open fan. From one corner protruded a short strip of metal, thin as ribbon.

Charley picked it up. "It's really light, whatever it is," he observed. He tapped the surface with a fingertip. "Definitely metal. Looks like gold, doesn't it?"

"It's brass, I think," Luciana said. "It's just been very well polished." Spying something, she leaned closer. There were three tiny indentations in the surface at each 'corner' of the fan shape. She took the object and held it up so that she could see the edge. Instead of being one flat piece of metal, it was actually formed of two very thin pieces held together. Sandwiched between the outer pieces were other pieces of metal.

"I think it opens," Luciana said.

They took turns trying to find a way to make it reveal its insides, but to no avail. There seemed to be no catch, no button, no hidden pressure point and no hinges. At last Luciana laid it on the floor between them.

"So … is this it?" Charley asked. "Is this the Golden Butterfly?"

Luciana sighed. "I don't know. It does almost look like a wing, doesn't it? But the Golden Butterfly was about levitation. My grandfather made his assistant fly up from the stage and vanish. I can't see how this lump of metal could help him do that, can you?"

"Whatever it is, it must be important," Charley said. "Marko hid it really well. I wish he were here to ask."

"So do I," Luciana said, the elation of solving the desk's puzzle dwindling.

"What shall we do with it? Are you going to put it back in the secret drawer?"

Luciana considered. "No," she said. "I want to work out how it opens." She thought for a moment. "What we need is a magnifying glass. That might reveal something we can't see with our eyes alone – like how to open it." She got to her feet. "Grandmother has one she uses for needlework in the evenings. I'll go and get it – you take this back to the drawing room. It's a bit warmer in there. Besides…" she stopped, hesitating.

Charley raised an eyebrow. "You don't want your grandmother to find us in here, with whatever it is?"

"I just don't want anyone to take it away from us," she said. "Not yet. Not until we know what it is."

When she got back to the drawing room with the magnifying glass, they tried to persuade the strange object to open, but to no avail.

"Maybe we need something to jimmy it," Charley suggested. "Something thin enough to slide between the edges."

Luciana went to the table beside the fireplace and pulled open the drawer, looking for her grandfather's old letter opener. The ruined poster of the Magnificent

Marko still rested on the tabletop. Her eye was drawn to the two lines of text printed at the bottom of the poster. Luciana had barely even noticed them before – she'd always been more interested in the image of her grandfather. Now she stared, transfixed. Then she snatched up both parts of the poster.

"Look!" she said, pointing. Below the picture was a white space with bold black words. It read:

Tickets for all performances available only at the Peacock Theatre, Aldwych. See the Magnificent Marko in the most luxurious theatre in all of London!

"The Peacock Theatre!" Charley exclaimed. "Like the peacock butterfly on the desk! That's a bit of a coincidence, isn't it?"

"Maybe. Or perhaps it isn't a coincidence at all."

"But if it isn't –" Charley frowned – "then what does it mean?"

Luciana sighed. "I don't know."

The lunch bell rang, its loud tinkle echoing up the stairs, accompanied by Isabella's voice.

"Luciana? Charley? Lunch is on the table," she called.

"Come on," Luciana said, hurriedly thrusting the device back into its pouch and looking around for somewhere to hide it. After a moment's hesitation, she put it behind the cushion in her grandfather's old chair.

*

"Luciana, I think we need to have a talk," her grandmother said after supper that evening. "About Charley."

Luciana looked up from her book, surprised. "Why?" she asked. "What's he done?"

Isabella sighed. "He hasn't done anything."

Luciana closed her book, puzzled. "What then?"

They were sitting in the parlour, settled in their two familiar old armchairs. There was a fire burning in the grate and Luciana had forced herself into the room despite it, trying to cure herself of the fear that had settled on her shoulders. *You've done it once,* she kept telling herself. *You can do it again. It's nothing but a nightmare, and nightmares don't mean anything.* At the moment it was working, just as long as she didn't look directly at the flames. Every time she did she saw that awful writhing figure, the one that haunted her dreams.

Luciana had always loved this room, because it was so distinctly her grandmother's, in the same way that the study was so clearly her grandfather's. There was a cabinet in one corner, full of beautiful glass dishes tinted the colour of the roses that bloomed over the door of the vicarage in summer. Her grandmother had told her once that they had been handed down to her through

39

generations and would one day belong to Luciana herself. There were paintings on the walls too, of elegant ladies with their hair done in elaborate styles. Each one was a distant ancestor, and when she'd been younger she had spent hours staring up at them, imagining herself in their extraordinary clothes and hats.

Now her grandmother was staring into the fire. She seemed to be weighing her words carefully.

"When you first came to us," she began, "I ... didn't know what to do. It was such a late age to be caring for a young child. Our friends' children were all grown up. Marko and I were both worried that you wouldn't have playmates of your own age. And besides, I felt that I needed help. Reverend Alders told us that his housekeeper, Agnes, had herself just had a child, and suggested that it could be a solution for the two of you to meet. I wasn't sure at first, but right from the start, even before either of you could walk, it seemed you were destined to be friends. Charley's mother put him down on that old rug in the drawing room next to you, and you looked at each other and laughed, and that was it."

Luciana smiled. "I am so glad that the Reverend had the idea," she said. "I must thank him the next time I see him. I can't imagine life without Charley in it."

Her grandmother's face took on an uncomfortable

expression. "I know, and that's what worries me, Luciana," she said. "I was so grateful not to be alone in the mission of raising you that I relied on Charley's visits too much. Soon he was here every day, almost as much a part of the household as you were. Marko loved it too. He was never happier than when he could hear the two of you laughing at whatever game you had dreamed up. We got so used to hearing two sets of footsteps chasing up and down the stairs in this house that it seemed entirely normal. But we shouldn't have let it carry on for so long. We shouldn't have let it become so familiar."

"But he's my friend," Luciana said. "He's my *best* friend. He's a good boy, you're always saying so."

Her grandmother sighed and passed one thin hand across her eyes. "He *is* a good boy, and I love him very much, but... You are both getting older now. You are thirteen. Soon you will no longer be children. And you must have noticed the differences in your situations."

"Our ... situations?" Luciana repeated, mystified.

"Charley's mother is the vicar's housekeeper, Luciana. They share an attic room, like any of the other vicarage servants. Soon he will have to go out to work himself – Mr Timms is already training him as a groundsman with a view to that being his profession. You, on the other hand..."

"You're saying that Charley and I can't be friends?" she asked. "Just because he doesn't have as much money as we do?"

Her grandmother sighed. "I am saying that your lives are on different paths, and always have been. I am saying that sooner or later those paths will diverge, and that it may be better for you both to not be so in step when they do."

Luciana did not answer. Her gaze had blurred. "Did Grandfather think the same way?"

Her grandmother was silent for a moment. "We … discussed it. He understood my concerns. And now the Magnificent Marko is gone and life must go on. I want you to have a good life, Luciana – a safe life, a secure life."

Luciana thought about this for a while, staring at the fire crackling in the grate. For the first time since Thursby's visit she was not afraid to look directly at it; its flame matched the burning feeling in her heart. Then she stood up and walked to the door.

"Luciana," her grandmother said. "You understand that I have nothing against Charley, and I do not mean that you have to stop seeing him completely, just—"

Luciana turned. "Charley isn't just my friend," she said. "He's my brother. He's always been my brother. He will always *be* my brother. Grandfather understood that,

I think. And that's all there is to it."

She left the parlour and went to her room. Luciana stayed there for the rest of the evening, thinking hard.

Chapter Six

Luciana spent the whole of the next day thinking through everything that had happened since Marko had died, and found herself forming an idea that could not be shifted. After all, until yesterday there had been only two people who had known that the secret drawer in the Magnificent Marko's desk existed – the man who had made it and her grandfather. With her solving of the puzzle, Charley and Luciana made four. Four people in the whole world who knew the secret! When she thought back carefully, Luciana had realized that it was only after her first discovery of the desk's concealed puzzle that her grandfather had begun to be really serious about teaching her how to identify his beloved butterflies. Surely the reason that her grandfather had been so keen to teach her about butterflies in the first place was so that she alone could decipher his puzzle? And if that was the case, how could she rest until she'd untangled the truth of what the mysterious device was?

Besides, the more Luciana thought about it, the more she was convinced that the device they had found *had* to have something to do with the Golden Butterfly. It was too much of a coincidence that she had been able to solve the puzzle that had led her to the device just a day after Thursby and his cronies had come searching for her grandfather's last and greatest trick. The two things had to be connected. She just had to work out how. Once she did, Luciana was convinced that she'd also learn the truth of what Thursby had done to make her grandfather leave the stage.

What she needed was someone who could tell her what the device was and what it was for, and there was only one place she could think of where such a person might exist. So it was that early on Friday morning, before the sun was even up, Luciana was watching out of the window for Charley. She saw him leave the vicarage and instead of waiting for him to arrive, she pulled on her coat and boots and went out to meet him.

It was February and England was still in the depths of winter. Snow had been pelting the village for days, and this morning it had begun again. Still, Luciana barely noticed as she forged her way through the orchard. The trees drooped beneath their burden, bare branches bending towards the ground as Luciana crunched her way beneath them.

Charley saw her coming and waved.

"Hello!" he called. "Fancied a walk?"

"I need to talk to you," she called back.

They met at the stream. The splash and tinkle of the water seemed loud in the cold air.

"What is it?" Charley asked with a laugh. "You look as if you've discovered all the gold of the Incas in your attic!"

"I know what we need to do," Luciana said, breathless. "We need to go to London. We need to go to the Peacock Theatre! It's obvious, isn't it?"

Charley looked shocked. "You want to go to *London*?"

"Of course! My grandfather performed there for years. If the answer to what the device is and how it fits in with the Golden Butterfly and Thursby is anywhere, it's there."

"How will we get there?" Charley asked, looking unconvinced.

"We'll catch a train," Luciana said impatiently. "The way

we used to when we were younger. Don't you remember?"

"I only went with you once," Charley told her. "When it was your birthday and you said that you wanted me to be allowed to come with you."

Luciana blinked in surprise. "Really?"

Charley nodded. "Really."

"I thought you came with us all the time," she said with a frown.

"I only came that time because your grandma and grandpa paid for my train ticket," Charley added. "It was far more money than my mother had to spare. And what about the carriage at the other end?"

"The carriage?"

"I remember there was a carriage waiting for us at the station. It took us straight to the theatre and then it took us back to the station again afterwards. Maybe we could walk from the station and back … but I don't know the way to the theatre, do you? Or how long it would take."

Luciana bit her lip. "I hadn't thought about any of that."

"I've got a little bit of money saved," Charley said. "From my work with Mr Timms. What I've got might be enough for part of a ticket. But probably not all of it."

Luciana looked down at the stream beside which they stood, the water glinting against the glare of the white snow as it tumbled over the rocks. Her grandmother's words echoed in her head. *Surely you must have noticed the difference in your situations.* Luciana pushed them away. She didn't want to think about the future her grandmother had suggested was just around the corner, especially if it was one without her best friend.

"I haven't got any money either," she said. "Whenever I need something, Grandmother gives it to me or takes me shopping. But I can't ask her for this – she'd never allow us to go alone and she won't take us herself, not once she knows why I want to go."

They stood in silence for a few minutes. Somewhere in the trees a pair of ravens croaked and bickered about the cold. Luciana watched Charley as he frowned, deep in thought about something. His face was so familiar – she couldn't imagine not seeing it every day. Her grandmother's words tried to force their way back into Luciana's head, and for a moment she wondered if she should tell Charley what Isabella had said. But she couldn't bring herself to say the words. She knew how upset he would be and besides, talking about it would just make it more real.

"I know a way we could earn the money," Charley said eventually. "My mother wouldn't approve and your grandmother certainly wouldn't, but it would work."

"What is it?"

"How many of your grandfather's card tricks do you know?"

"Twenty or thirty, perhaps. Why?"

Charley hitched up his bag and slung it over his shoulder. "You could perform them for money."

Luciana frowned. "Where would I find a theatre willing to take me on?"

"You don't need a theatre. You just need a busy street. It's Saturday tomorrow, which means it's market day in Rotherton. The square there will be full. I bet you could gather a crowd. We'd ask them for a penny – or no, not even that – a ha'penny – each."

It was Luciana's turn to be doubtful. "You really think they would pay?"

"Definitely," Charley said, his enthusiasm building as he warmed to the idea. "People love magic. And the idea of a girl performing it – that's so strange they won't be able to stay away. I can be the money-gatherer. I'll tell them that if they're not amazed, we'll give them double their money back!"

"Oh, I'm not sure that's a good idea…"

"It is. It's a great idea," Charley insisted. "I have faith in you, Ana. You can do it."

Luciana swallowed hard. Standing up in front of a crowd? She'd never performed in front of more than one or two people before, and they were always the same ones – the Magnificent Marko, her grandmother and Charley. The thought of a mass of people she didn't know, all watching her … her hands shook just thinking about it. And yet what was the alternative? If they were going to go to London, they needed the money, and as far as Luciana could see, there was no other way to get it. She took a deep breath.

"All right," she said. "Tell me how this is going to work."

*

At 5 a.m. on Saturday morning, Luciana slipped out of her bedroom and made her way downstairs. In the cloakroom she quickly pulled on her boots and the warmest of her winter coats. Then she crept out of the kitchen door. Luciana was anxious that she was already late. She had tarried too long over the writing of the note that she hoped would stop her grandmother worrying.

Over her shoulder she carried a soft cotton patchwork bag. Inside were two decks of cards – an old pack her grandfather had given her and an unopened one that she had taken from the drawer in his desk. Every time he performed, Marko would open a new deck, and the habit of maintaining a full stock had never left him. Also in the bag was a large piece of fruitcake that Luciana had saved from her supper the night before, two apples, two changes of underclothes and the golden device, secure in its black velvet pouch.

Luciana hurried down the path that cut through the forest above the village, trying to avoid the deepest of the snow. Charley was waiting for her beside the vicarage gate, hidden in the winter pre-dawn darkness, given away only by the puff of his breath. At the sound of her footsteps he peeked out and beckoned her to be quicker. Luciana dashed across the road and ducked under the snowy bower of the holly bush. As she did, the tell-tale double clip-clop of a horse and cart sounded in the distance, drawing rapidly closer.

"All right," Charley said. "Here's what's going to happen. Mr Dewson will be driving, with his boy Will to help him with the goods. They'll pull up at the gate and take down the sacks of flour and potatoes that Mrs Grouse ordered yesterday – they always drop off our orders on their way to market. They'll carry them round to the kitchen door. While they're doing that, you and I must get on the back of the wagon and hide."

"Won't they see us as soon as they come back to the cart?" Luciana asked in a whisper, as the clatter of hooves drew ever nearer.

"The goods will be covered by a blanket," said Charley.

"We just need to get under it. I'll give you a boost up first, and then I'll follow. All right?"

Luciana took a deep breath as the cart pulled to a halt in the gloom beyond the gate. "All right," she said.

Chapter Seven

Rotherton was a small town about twice the size of Midford, five miles away. Whereas Midford had only a post office and Mr Smith the grocer's shop, Rotherton had a milliner and a dressmaker's, a saddlery, a restaurant, a bank, two public houses, its own grocery and post office, and Mr Thacker's dusty bookshop. These were all crowded around the town square, which on Saturdays filled with market stalls and the hustle and bustle of produce and livestock sellers from the surrounding villages.

Luciana and Charley's journey that cold morning was bumpy and uncomfortable. Crammed between crates and sacks, the stowaways felt every hole in the uneven road.

"When we stop," Charley whispered, "we need to slip

out as quickly as we can, before they pull the blanket back and start unloading. Stay low and follow me. Be ready to run if we need to, all right?"

"I'm ready," Luciana whispered back, nervous but excited. It certainly beat sitting at home, pricking her fingers with embroidery needles. She was a little worried though, as it seemed a storm was brewing. She wondered if they were about to be confronted by a downpour that would turn the snow to slush.

Then the cart turned a corner and Luciana realized that the sound she had thought was thunder rumbling in the distance was actually the noise of many people. The hubbub grew louder as the cart slowed. Shouts emanated from not far above the blanket: it was Mr Dewson's voice.

"Out the way! Coming through! Watch yer back, won't yer?"

"Hold yer horsefeathers!" shouted another voice, "T'aint nobody 'ere's fault that you're late but yourn, is it?"

There was a bit more back and forth as the cart edged its way forward so slowly that it would probably have been quicker to walk. Charley realized this too.

"Come on," he urged her. "If we can hop off now, all the better!"

Charley shuffled to the edge of the blanket, hitched it

up and vanished over the end of the cart. A second later his head reappeared.

"Quick, now!" he hissed, "Before someone sees!"

Luciana crawled towards him, dragging her bag behind her and struggling against the rocking of the cart. Charley grabbed her arms and pulled her to the ground, holding her upright to stop her stumbling. They both looked around – Luciana was sure that someone must have seen them, but no one had taken any notice. The whole place was crowded with people and alive with movement.

Charley grabbed her hand as the roiling crowd swallowed them up. Luciana almost fell over a goose, which squawked angrily at her, snapping at her ankles as she danced hurriedly out of the way. Dogs and children darted through the trodden snow. Several times Luciana had to dodge boxes and crates being passed over her head, laden with everything from fish still gasping for breath to crates of kindling and boxes of tea. The air was full of the smells of roasting chestnuts, horses, fresh bread, crushed dried herbs, burning charcoal and who knew what else. By the time they reached the other side of the square, Luciana's head was spinning and she was out of breath.

"We'll be fine now," said Charley, stopping. "Mr Dewson will be none the wiser. And look, we've found the perfect place for you to perform."

Luciana looked around, nerves bubbling. She'd had no idea there would be so many people here. She wasn't sure she could stop her hands shaking long enough to get her cards out of her bag, let alone perform sleight of hand.

"Hey," Charley said, squeezing her shoulder. "You're going to be fine. You can do this. And after all—"

"I know," she said, taking a deep breath. "If I want to get to London, this is the only way. I'm fine. I promise."

"Good. Better get ready: the sooner we get started, the sooner we'll have earned enough to hop on a train."

Ignoring the hammering of her heart, Luciana pulled her bag from her shoulder. Looking down at herself she realized she had bits of hay and dust stuck all over her from the cart ride, and her boots were soaked with snowmelt. She brushed off what she could, pulled her coat straight, stamped both her feet once to rid them of snow, and looked Charley in the eye.

"All right then," she said. "How do we begin?"

Charley raised an eyebrow and grinned, then spun away from her.

"Ladies and gents," he called loudly into the even louder crowd. "Ladies and gents, come on now – roll up, roll up for the greatest show you've ever seen!"

Luciana's heart turned over. She scrabbled to take out the open deck of cards.

"You what?" said a large and formidable man in a grubby butcher's tunic, as he towered over Charley. "What are you up to, you dirty little urchin?"

"Ahh, now, sir," Charley said with an extravagant bow. "You look like the discerning type. For no more than a ha'penny, you can see some of the most astonishing magic around."

"Oh yeah?" The man said with a deep, booming guffaw. "You going to try to con me with the three-card trick are you? Think I was born yesterday, you young scallywag? I'll call the law on you, sonny Jim!"

"It's not the three-card trick, sir, nor anything like it. It's not fraud, nor theft, nor cheatery of any kind," Charley insisted with another flourish. "It's magic, pure and simple."

The man snorted, one meaty fist on one meaty hip, the other digging in his pocket from where he pulled a dull copper coin. "Magic, my big bumcheeks. All right then, show me what you've got."

"Oh, I don't have a magical bone in my body, sir," Charley said, whipping off his cap for the butcher to drop the ha'penny into. He swept his arm in an arc to indicate Luciana. "It's the young lady here who will amaze you."

The butcher's gaze flicked to where Luciana stood. He took her in with a glance, in much the same way that

Thursby had. It was a look of disdain, of disinterest, of disbelief. A second later the man boomed a mocking laugh.

"Pull the other one, you scoundrel!" he exclaimed. "As if some silly little girl could do something to amaze me! A *girl*! Don't waste my time. Here, give me back my ha'penny afore I really do call the law on yer."

At the man's word's, Luciana was suddenly angry, filled with an indignant fury. *How dare he?* she thought. *How DARE he? I'll show him.*

Luciana began to move the cards. She fanned them and shuffled them, she passed them from one hand to another in a long continuous line that seemed to move of its own accord. A hush fell over the crowd.

"'Ere," said the butcher. "That ain't natural. That ain't *proper*. Time was she'd be burned as a witch, doing things like that."

"Aha," said Charley, quick as a flash. "So you're already prepared to admit that what you're seeing is magic, sir, as performed by the young lady? You're ready to forfeit your ha'penny?"

"No, ain't saying that," blustered the man. "I ain't saying that at all."

"Well then," said Charley, holding out his cap. "Let's see if anyone else agrees. Or perhaps you've all seen enough already? A ha'penny, that's all we're asking. Can't say fairer than that, can we, ladies and gents?"

Charley's cap began to fill. He glanced over at Luciana with a flick of his eyebrow and she took that as her cue to begin.

Chapter Eight

"So how much money have we got after buying the tickets?" Luciana asked later, once they were settled on the train.

"Six shillings, threepence ha'penny," Charley said, beginning to collect the coins he'd been counting out on to the seat beside him. "I don't know if that's enough for somewhere to stay."

"Let's worry about that if we have to," said Luciana, reaching into her bag and pulling out the apples, one of which she passed to Charley. "We might be able to get back home tonight anyway."

Charley nodded, and for a time there was no sound in the carriage apart from the crunch as they ate and the *rittle-rattle, rittle-rattle* of the train's wheels over the tracks. Outside, the winter sun was still rising in the sky. The whole day stretched ahead of them and Luciana felt nothing but excitement.

The train pulled into Charing Cross station just after 1 p.m. They pushed open the door of their carriage and stumbled down on to a platform wreathed in chaos and saturated by steam and soot – Luciana was immediately engulfed by memory. It was a few years since she'd last arrived in the station, but it was such a familiar scene that a lump formed in her throat. Travellers wrestled with luggage amid the greasy air, porters scurried this way and that, trains came and went with their conductors hollering to one another as the piercing whistles of their engines did the same. Luciana loved the noise and bustle, even though this time her grandfather would not be waiting at the end of the journey to scoop her up into a hug.

They began to make their way along the platform, and Luciana was relieved that neither she nor Charley had brought more with them. She held her bag tight, continually checking through the fabric to make sure that the device inside the little velvet pouch was still there.

"I think the exit is that way," Luciana said, pointing towards the great exodus of people pushing towards two wide corridors either side of the ticket booths.

"Wait," Charley said. "Perhaps we should ask someone for directions."

"Carry yer luggage, ladies and gents?" came a thin, high voice somewhere just south of Charley's shoulder. "Reasonable prices! Carry yer luggage to yer hotel. No dropping guaranteed!"

The owner of the voice was a small scrawny boy in a tweed cap several degrees more battered than Charley's own. He was threading through the crowds and every now and then he'd peer upwards and his sly fingers would slip towards a gaping pocket before vanishing again, quick as you like.

"Oi," called Charley. "You, boy – c'mere."

The boy gave Charley a quick look up and down. "All right, guv'nor?" he said. "What can I do you for? Carry yer luggage, shall I?"

"No," said Charley. "We need you to take us to an address. Can you do that?"

The boy sniffed and wiped the back of his grubby hand across his nose. "Depends," he said.

"Depends on what?" Luciana asked.

"On where it is and what yer planning to give me in readies," he said. "I ain't keen on going sarf o' the river, fer a start."

"The Peacock Theatre is where we need to go," Luciana told him. "Can you help us? We can spare a shilling."

The boy perked up. "Oh, aye," he said. "I can take you

to the Peacock, no probs." He held out one dirty hand. "A shilling's fair enough – long as I get it up front, like."

Charley reached into his pocket and scooped out a handful of ha'pennies before counting twenty-four into the boy's cupped palm. The boy wrinkled his nose at the heap of copper. Then he gave a quick shrug and shoved the coins into his pockets.

"Ah well," he said. "Money's money, ain't it? Come on then."

He took off through the crowds, leaving Luciana and Charley struggling to keep up.

*

It turned out that the Peacock Theatre was just fifteen minutes' walk from Charing Cross station. Their guide took them out into the smoggy city air, through the wrought-iron enclosure of the station's forecourt, and immediately turned right on to the Strand. From there it was no more than a stroll up the straight, wide thoroughfare, with a left turn into a crescent of tall buildings.

"'Ere we is," the boy said smartly, drawing to a stop outside the splendid façade that Luciana remembered so well. "The Peacock, safe and sound. Now I got to trot, quick as – don't want to miss the two o'clock comin' in from Tunbridge Wells. All right?"

"Thank you," Luciana called out after his retreating back, but he had already vanished into the throngs of people that lined the street. She turned back to the theatre, lost once again in memories of previous visits.

"It doesn't look very open," Charley said, noting the locked doors and darkened windows.

"It isn't," Luciana agreed. "The box office for this evening's show won't open until at least five o'clock."

"You mean we have to wait until then?" Charley asked, dismayed.

"Definitely not," Luciana reassured him. "Come on, it's this way."

She led him towards a dim alleyway that snaked around the side of the theatre. Set in the wall halfway down was a wide black door that was beginning to peel. Above it was a stained-glass panel. It was constructed from shards of yellow glass, but at its centre, picked out in dull red hues, were the words 'Stage Door'. To one side of the door hung a rope with a loop of frayed fabric at the end. Luciana reached out and pulled it, hard. From inside the still and silent building came the distant jangle of a ringing bell.

Luciana and Charley stood there waiting. Nothing happened. The ringing bell settled itself. Frowning a little, Luciana pulled at the rope again.

"Perhaps there's no one here?" Charley asked.

"There must be," Luciana told him. "There's always *someone* at a theatre."

Still no one came. In fact it took four rings of the ancient bell before the sound of footsteps echoed from within. As they neared, so too did a voice uttering a stream of curses that grew ever louder.

Luciana stepped away as several bolts were thrust back, her confidence slipping a little as the muffled tirade continued. Finally the door was thrown open to reveal a small rotund man with a dishevelled handlebar moustache and thinning hair that had been combed across a bare dome of a forehead.

"What in the blazes are you doing, ring-ring-ringing at that bell in broad daylight?" he roared. "Why can't it wait until we are actually open? Since I am not advertising any vacant positions, I have no need of a shoeshine and I most definitely do not want to find God, it is beyond my powers of imagination!"

For a moment there was utter silence. This was not the welcome Luciana had anticipated. Every other visit to her grandfather's theatre had been a whirlwind of wonder and laughter. True, she had not expected that everyone would recognize her after so many years away, but the vehemence of this greeting pushed all the words Luciana had prepared straight out of her head.

"Right," huffed the man. "Well then, I'll thank you to clear off and leave a man to his well-earned lunchtime rest!"

He went to close the door. In a flash of desperation, Luciana cried out.

"Oh, but Mr Hibberd! It's me! It's Luciana Cattaneo! I just want to talk to you for a moment, that's all!"

But the door was already in motion. It slammed in their faces.

Chapter Nine

"Come on," Charley said after another moment, sounding as deflated as Luciana felt. "Let's not just stand here. Let's—"

The door was flung open again. Once again, Mr Hibberd filled the doorway, but this time the look on his face was of utter astonishment.

"Cattaneo?" He enquired loudly. "Luciana Cattaneo? Is it truly you? But it cannot be! I used to bounce you on my knee when you were nothing but a dot!"

Luciana's heart had yet to regain its normal pace, but she managed to nod. "Yes, Mr Hibberd. I remember. You used to save me bits of the cake your wife made you for lunch."

Mr Hibberd emitted a sudden, loud guffaw. The sound made Luciana smile, for she remembered it, as much as she remembered that everything she had seen of Mr Hibberd in the past five minutes was perfectly indicative of the man's character. He was larger than life, as a man of the theatre should most definitely be.

"Well, I never did!" he said, throwing his arms wide. "I never thought to see you again, and look here – so grown up! Come in, my dear, and your companion too. What a very long time it has been!"

Mr John Hibberd, the long-standing building manager of the Peacock Theatre, took Luciana and Charley into the room where he spent most of his time. Being below street level, it was lit by an oil lamp that rendered the room dim and the air clogged even in the middle of the day. In one corner stood a large and comfortable armchair. In front of it was a small footrest, and on the floor beside it was a discarded blanket. The rest of the room was in a similar state of disarray, from the desk that was covered with piles of papers, books and posters, to the coat rack in another corner that seemed so laden it might topple over at any moment.

"Make yourselves at home, my dears, while I find some more chairs and light the stove for some tea."

Over tea they discovered that Mr Hibberd did not

know about the death of the Magnificent Marko.

"I am so sorry, Mr Hibberd," Luciana said. "I assumed you would know."

Mr Hibberd retrieved a creased kerchief from his top pocket and dabbed at his eyes with it. "No, my dear," he said. "I had not heard. But then, we none of us had heard a peep from the great master of magic ever since he withdrew from the stage. Such a shame, that was, such an awful, terrible shame. There will never be another like your grandfather, Miss Cattaneo. He lit up the stage with a fire of the kind that had never been seen before and surely will never be seen again. In fact, with his departure went the golden age of magic in England. It has been fading ever since, like a flower past its best. We haven't had a magician here since he left the stage, you know. There are fewer and fewer of them about."

Luciana glanced at Charley and then said, "Mr Hibberd, I am going to be honest with you now, because I believe I can trust you."

The theatre man looked at her, eyes bulging a little in surprise. "But of course you can, my dear. Your grandfather could always rely on my discretion and support, and of course I will forever extend the same to you."

Luciana smiled. "I am very grateful to hear you say that. You see, Charley and I are on the trail of a mystery, and we

69

came here in the hope that a visit may help us to unravel it."

"A mystery!" Hibberd repeated in astonishment that seemed to Luciana to be tinged with excitement. "To do with the Magnificent Marko, you mean?"

"Yes," said Luciana. "Mr Hibberd, can you tell me anything about a man called Thursby?"

The look that settled on Mr Hibberd's face took her by surprise, not least because it so closely matched the one she had seen on her grandmother's when confronted by the man himself.

"Thursby," rumbled Mr Hibberd angrily. "That demon in a man's guise. Oh yes. I can tell you about *him*."

"Who is he?" Luciana asked. "My grandmother could not even bring herself to tell me that."

"Ah, well," said Mr Hibberd, "a sensible precaution, for who would want to summon the devil by describing him? I shall risk it, however. Carl Thursby is the Master of the Grand Society of Magicians."

There was a pause. Mr Hibberd had announced this as if it had been accompanied by a drum roll.

"I never knew there was such a thing," said Charley. "The Grand Society of Magicians, I mean. It sounds very ... grand."

"Oh, it is, young man," said Hibberd. "Grand and

extremely important. Or it used to be at any rate. No magician in England can perform magic in public without being a member and holding a licence to do so. The Society decides who is fit to be on the stage: who, indeed, may use the name 'magician'."

"I see," said Luciana slowly. "How do they do that, exactly?"

"Each magician must apply for his licence and must prove himself fit to hold it by pledging to uphold the Society's laws. It is a most grave offence for a licensed magician to disgrace himself by breaking any one of them and doing so means immediate rejection from the Society."

Luciana stared into her empty teacup, watching the tea leaves as they settled in their patterns at its base. "I suppose … that loss also means the loss of earnings – of livelihood. If a magician cannot perform."

"Absolutely," agreed Hibberd. "It is a most terrible situation. I can only think of it ever happening once in my memory, in fact."

"My grandfather," Luciana said, her mouth growing dry. "He lost his licence, didn't he? That's why he left the stage?"

A sad frown passed over Mr Hibberd's face. "Yes. And it was Thursby who masterminded his downfall. And let me tell you, it might be the first time he'd got a fellow thrown

71

out of the Society, but the scuttlebutt is that it isn't the first time he's got rid of a rival by nefarious means."

Luciana felt a cold pit open up in her belly. "What happened? I want to understand. What magician's law was my grandfather accused of breaking?"

"Thursby accused him of teaching the secrets of magic to a non-magician."

Luciana was confused. "What does that mean, exactly?"

Mr Hibberd shrugged. "Only licensed magicians are permitted to know the secrets behind performing magic. One is first granted an apprentice's licence, then a full licence once a commitment to the profession is proven. It helps to keep the profession streamlined. If just anyone could learn, where would we be then, eh? We'd be overrun with amateurs and then why would anyone pay to come to a theatre? You'd have cheap tricksters performing on every street corner for a measly handful of coins!"

Luciana and Charley looked at each other with alarm. "Who was my grandfather accused of teaching?"

"Ah, well. That's where it becomes murky," said Hibberd, apparently oblivious to their discomfort. "He was accused of teaching his assistant, Adeline Morrell. Do you remember her?"

Luciana frowned. "I saw her on stage with my grandfather, of course. I can't recall ever meeting her properly though."

"She was a very clever girl, a very good magician's assistant, and this is where Thursby showed his true snake-in-the-grass nature. Because there has always been a grey area when it comes to magicians and their assistants. Every assistant is herself a member of the Society and there is an understanding. After all, how is an assistant to assist her master without knowing at least *some* of what goes into his routines? So in that sense, the Magnificent Marko probably *had* taught some of his magic to Adeline. But no magician had ever been held up against the laws of the Society for that. Not until –" and here Hibberd fairly spat the name – "*Thursby*. He saw a way of getting rid of Marko and he took it."

Luciana was finding it more and more difficult to breathe. After all, Marko had always taught magic to *her*. "Then … perhaps the accusation was because he was also teaching another?"

"Oh no," Hibberd said with utmost confidence. "It was Adeline all right. It was because of the Golden Butterfly. And of course the whole debacle wasn't really about the rules at all. It was about Thursby wanting that trick. He was infuriated that he could not copy it. He'd love to be able to call himself the greatest magician of the age, but he doesn't have the talent. He has lied, bullied and bought his way into the power he has, and he has done the same to diminish every magician better than he – which is all of them. If magic is dying, then he is the sickness killing it. At first he tried to steal the Golden Butterfly, as he did with all his other tricks, and when he could not, he resolved to force your grandfather from the stage so that at least no one was performing it. The accusation of teaching Adeline was what it took."

Luciana's head was spinning. She couldn't even begin to make sense of what Hibberd was telling them. "But I thought you said that Adeline Morrell was also a member of the Society?"

"Oh yes, of course. She was registered as an assistant."

Charley cleared his throat. "The Golden Butterfly," he said. "That's what Thursby and his men were looking for when they turned up at Luciana's home on the day of the funeral."

"*What?*" Hibberd asked, aghast. "My God, the sheer nerve of the man, to disturb a grieving family. What *evil*!"

"He didn't find it," Luciana told him.

"Well, thank heaven for small mercies," said Hibberd. "That really would be the icing on the cake, to have that damnable slug crowing from the paste-boards that he was to revive the Golden Butterfly."

"But ... but I think *we* might have," she added. Reaching for her bag, Luciana pulled from it the velvet pouch and drew out the triangle of golden metal. She passed it to Mr Hibberd in silence. "Or part of it anyway. This was hidden in my grandfather's study," Luciana said. "We don't know what it is. Do you think this is what Thursby was looking for?"

Mr Hibberd turned the device over in his hands for a few moments, then handed it back with a shake of his head. "Possibly, my dear, but I really could not say." He smiled wistfully. "Of course, I never have been privy to the secrets of the magicians' world, not even with all the years I've spent looking after this place."

Luciana slipped the golden wing back into its pouch. "I suppose the person who could tell us is Adeline Morrell. Do you know where she is?"

"No idea, I'm afraid. Magicians are a superstitious bunch, even more so than stage folk in general. No one would employ her after she was caught up in that scandal."

"If she supposedly knew the secret of how to perform the Golden Butterfly," Charley asked thoughtfully, "then why didn't she? Later, I mean, once the Magnificent Marko had left the stage? She could have carried on."

"Yes, why didn't she just do it herself?" Luciana asked.

Hibberd stared at her for a moment, and then burst out laughing. "Oh, my dear," he said, "you have such comportment that for a moment I clean forgot that you are

75

still a child, with the capacity to say things of such hilarity. Of course she could not do that."

"But why not?" Luciana asked, still confused.

Hibberd stopped laughing, as if only realizing then that she was asking a genuine question. "Why, women cannot perform magic, my dear."

Chapter Ten

The idea that women could not perform magic made no sense to Luciana. After all, if that was the case, what exactly was it that she herself had been doing in that crowded market square in Rotherton not six hours earlier? Perhaps, she thought, what Mr Hibberd actually meant was not that women *could not* perform magic, but merely that they were not *allowed* to perform magic. Although that seemed as absurd as the idea that women could not perform magic at all.

"But then – what was the point of Adeline being a member of the Grand Society?" Luciana asked.

"Well, of course," Mr Hibberd said, "every magician's assistant must be licensed themselves. They have their own separate list. It is a very great honour to be admitted," he said, leaning forward a little, as if he was somehow giving her a gift. "The assistants are very lucky. Each and every magician must prove himself worthy, no matter his parentage. But with assistants – each new daughter born is automatically inducted as a member. It's an acknowledgment, you know, of how hard they work."

"But they are not allowed to perform magic themselves."

Mr Hibberd leaned back with another huff of laughter. "Why, my dear, it is well known that a woman's mind does not possess the necessary levels of natural intelligence that are required to master the magical arts."

Luciana nodded absently as the words of the dismissive butcher returned to her from that morning. "And yet," she said quietly, "a few hundred years ago they were burned as witches. Is that not strange?"

There was a short silence, during which Mr Hibberd shifted uncomfortably in his seat. Luciana looked over at Charley. He shrugged and then glanced down at her bag. She knew what he was suggesting – that she should get out her cards and demonstrate just what a woman's mind was capable of. Luciana wondered what Mr Hibberd's reaction would be.

"Well," said the man. "Perhaps there is wisdom there too. Who knows what dangers a woman would be opening her mind to were she to push its capacities beyond its natural boundaries? All manner of evil could find its way in to corrupt her gentleness. But as *helpers*, they are unparalleled. Miss Morrell, for example, was the best in the business by far. I will readily admit that without her, I am sure the Golden Butterfly would not have been such a spectacle. Such a pity that she vanished from our esteemed London stages."

"There's no hope that we might be able to find her?" Charley asked. "Perhaps she would be able to explain the importance of this device."

Mr Hibberd waved a dismissive hand. "Oh, I'm sure if she ever knew, she'd have forgotten by now. Besides which, she will only have known in the very vaguest terms, enough to make the trick work. She will be somewhere abroad – far enough away that she can find another position and use for her talents without the scandal following her. Performing folk really are a peculiar bunch. Why, did you know that no one will take your grandfather's dressing room, even now? No one has touched it since he departed."

Luciana started in surprise. "You mean – it's just as he left it?"

Mr Hibberd nodded. "Oh yes. I wrote to Mr Cattaneo a month or so after the incident, asking what I should do with everything still in the room. In his reply he said

I could dispose of everything as I saw fit, and he trusted me to forward anything that looked important. But it never felt right to throw anything away, and since no one ever wanted to occupy the room … well, I simply locked the door and left it as it was."

"Did Thursby's men ever search it?" Charley asked.

"Oh yes. Thursby came down himself with one of his lackeys the week after the final performance. He demanded the key and sent me away. I was watching as he left. His companion was carrying a box of various things – I saw papers and other oddments in there – but neither would tell me what they were or why they wanted them."

Luciana looked at Charley. "Whatever was in the box, it can't have been about the Golden Butterfly," she said. "Otherwise why would he have come to our house this many years later, still looking for it?"

Charley nodded, then looked at Mr Hibberd. "Could we see the room ourselves?"

"Of course," said Mr Hibberd with a generous smile.

*

Mr Hibberd turned the lock on the painted dark blue door and pushed it inwards.

"Wait just a moment," he said, disappearing inside. "I'll light the old oil lamp."

Luciana tried not to think about the flame that Hibberd had gone to light in the stuffy, dusty space beyond the door. *Everything is fine*, she told herself. *It's perfectly safe, just as much as a fire in a grate. You know it is.* To calm herself she focused on the door in front of her instead. It was so familiar. She could recall scampering towards it, excited to visit her grandfather after he'd stepped off stage. When she had been very young, she would reach up for the smooth silver doorknob. It had loomed above her head like a miniature moon. Then would come her grandmother's words, calling after her to admonish her to *always knock first*. From within, her grandfather's voice would call for her to enter, and a moment later she would find herself scooped up into his warm arms and hugged, hard. Often there would be others in the room too, ladies and gentlemen in theatre-going finery, admirers of the Magnificent Marko who had wished to meet the man in person. He'd always had time for her though. She had always come first.

A warm flower of light bloomed within.

"There now," came Mr Hibberd's voice. "Come in, come in."

Another flood of memories eddied around Luciana as she stepped over the threshold. At one end was an area half concealed by a folding screen. The space beyond it, she remembered, was where her grandfather had retired to change before and after each performance. Opposite, against the wall, was a dressing table and mirror where he would put on his stage rouge and arrange his hair.

In front of the screen were a chaise longue and two armchairs, set around a small occasional table inlaid with the pattern of a backgammon board – this was the area where he would entertain guests. Against the wall was another desk with its own chair. Luciana went to it, but it was too plain to hold a secret compartment. It had no hidden puzzles to solve.

Luciana knew instinctively that nothing here was going to help them understand what the device was. Her disappointment was acute and bitter. With Adeline Morrell out of reach too, perhaps, after all, they had had a wasted journey.

"I shall leave you a while," Mr Hibberd said, "let you mull over your memories. I have a few things to attend to upstairs."

He left, pulling the door shut behind him. Luciana and Charley looked at each other.

"There's nothing here," she said.

Charley smiled. She could tell he thought the same. "Still," he said. "We should search properly. Since we came all this way."

Luciana nodded. He was right, of course, and so they

examined every corner of the room and its dusty furniture. Charley even went to the lengths of carefully turning over the armchairs to check their feet for secret compartments, but there was nothing.

"Come on," Luciana said eventually, her dejection complete. "If we leave now, we could get the three o'clock train home and be back in time for supper."

She held open the door while he shut off the oil lamp. They were making their way back towards Mr Hibberd's office when Charley stopped. He looked back down the corridor with a slight frown on his face.

"What?" Luciana asked.

He looked at her. "What about Adeline Morrell's dressing room? Where was that?"

Luciana searched her memory and then pointed to a door on the left. "It was that one, I think."

"I'm just going to take a look," said Charley. "Since we're here."

"But hundreds of different people will have used it since she left. And if there was nothing helpful in my grandfather's room, how can there be anything in hers?"

"Just a quick look," Charley insisted.

Charley set off without waiting to hear her reply. Luciana hesitated for another moment and then followed. There would be nothing to see, she was sure of it, certainly nothing to help them decipher the meaning of the device.

Yet when she followed Charley through the unlocked door, Luciana was assaulted by a memory so powerful that she almost staggered under its weight.

Chapter Eleven

She was small, wrapped up in a coat too big for her. She knew this place as well as she knew anything in her little life. She walked as though walking was new, tottering, uncertain, zigzagging side-to-side, as if ready to fall over at any moment.

Luciana gasped.

"Ana?" Charley grabbed her arm to help her keep upright. "What is it?"

"I know this place," she said, her tone hushed, rasping in the stale air of the room.

"You mean from the times you used to visit your grandfather?" Charley said. "That makes sense, I suppose."

Luciana shook her head, confused. "No. That's not it." She took another step into the room. It was smaller and more sparsely furnished than her grandfather's. There was a double-length dressing table with an equally long mirror. Set between the thin legs were three plain wooden chairs with uncomfortable, upright backs. At the far end, large enough to take up the space from wall to wall, was a fitted wardrobe and in front of that a metal pole from which was hanging a heavy green velvet curtain.

Charley walked to the wardrobe and pulled open the double doors. Inside there was only a thin metal rail.

"Well, you were right," Charley said. "There's nothing here."

Luciana found herself frozen to the spot as another recollection pulled her along in its fierce undertow. She stared past him, into the empty wardrobe.

"Ana?" Charley's voice sounded far away. "Shall we go? If we hurry, we can still make the train…"

It was dark where she was, lit only by a narrow sliver of light. It was small, this space, but she wasn't afraid. It was warm and cosy. She had somewhere to sleep and even better, she had her favourite toy. All she had to do was keep quiet…

She walked past Charley, stepping right inside the empty wardrobe. Then she dropped to her knees. Luciana pressed her fingers to the bottom right-hand corner, where the rear of the wardrobe met its base. She dragged her fingers up, feeling for something she knew would be there. Her fingers found a smooth dip in the wood and she fitted the palm of her hand to it, pushing against it.

A panel clicked open, nothing more than four thin dark lines in the shape of a rectangle appearing in the white paint. It slid sideways to reveal a small compartment.

Charley was by her side in a second. "How did you know that was there? How did you know how to open it?"

"I don't know," she whispered.

They both peered into the little chamber. It was too small for either of them to get inside. As her eyes adjusted to the dimness, Luciana made out a soft shape. She knew without reaching for it that it was a pile of blankets. She pulled them towards her and as she did so, something concealed within them clunked along the floor. Lifting the blankets, Luciana picked up the object beneath, drawing it into the light as she sat back.

"What the blazes is that?" Charley asked.

Luciana held a rectangular box made of different-coloured panels of wood. Each panel was inlaid with radiating circles in a pattern that was no pattern, and at the centre of each of these circles was a small spur of wood.

"Wait a minute," said Charley. "We've seen this kind of thing before, haven't we?"

Luciana sat mutely, staring down at the strange box cradled in her lap. She felt as if she were falling into a very deep, dark hole. From a distance came the sound of footsteps echoing closer.

"Quick," Charley said. "I don't think we should show this to Mr Hibberd, do you?"

She pushed the box into her bag while Charley hurriedly slid the secret panel back into place. They stumbled out of the dressing room just as Mr Hibberd appeared at the end of the corridor.

"I thought we'd have a quick peek in Adeline Morrell's dressing room," Charley said cheerfully, as he neared. "Just in case. Nothing in there though."

"Oh no, you'd find nothing in there," agreed Mr Hibberd. "Too many pairs of feet in and out since she used the room, I'm afraid!"

"Did she ever come back?" Charley asked. "After the … incident, I mean?"

Mr Hibberd frowned thoughtfully. "Just once," he said. "About a month after the whole debacle. She said she thought she'd left a wrap in the dressing room and wanted to look for it. I told her there was nothing there, but she insisted on coming down here just the same. I think that perhaps she just wanted one last look at the place, for sentimental reasons. And that was it, I never saw her again."

"Well," said Luciana, regaining her voice. "Thank you for your time, Mr Hibberd, and for allowing us to wander around your theatre. We should be going now."

"Oh, are you sure?" the man asked, disappointed. "I was going to say that you should stay for tonight's performance. We've got a rather funny farce on at the moment. Doors slamming and what-not."

"Thank you, but we really must catch our train," said Charley, as he and Luciana began to make for the stage door, with Mr Hibberd following behind. "If we hurry, we can still make it."

The three of them bid a swift goodbye at the door, with Mr Hibberd procuring from them the promise of a return in the future. He waved from the artiste's entrance until they got to the end of the passageway and had turned into the late afternoon bustle of Aldwych.

"We can't go straight home," Luciana said, once they were away from the theatre. "This is another puzzle – I've got to try to solve it."

"All right," said Charley, looking around. Across the wide road he saw a sign for a 'Mudie's Select Library'. "Let's go in there."

They dodged their way across the busy thoroughfare and pushed open the heavy wooden door. Inside the entrance there was a large plain oak desk, behind which sat a white-haired librarian in a stern black suit. Beyond was a large room that smelled of books. Crowded bookshelves lined the walls and reached up into the vaulted ceiling, accessed by moving ladders that slid to and fro on runners. The centre of the space held more bookshelves that formed narrow corridors. High above, the roof was made of small panels of thick glass that let in the dull February light. The place was very quiet, though a few people were wandering about, choosing books.

Luciana and Charley smiled at the librarian, who looked at them suspiciously but didn't stop them from coming in. Together they slipped right to the back of the library, where a table stood surrounded by hard-backed chairs. They sat down and Luciana pulled out the box.

They both looked at it. Four of the sides had the same kind of nonsensical mess of circles, dots and panels. Luciana picked it up with both hands and some deep memory bubbled to the surface of her mind. She knew how this worked. She had played with this box before, even though she had forgotten it entirely until she'd picked it up again. She turned both ends of the box in opposite directions, and the panels moved. Some of them rotated clockwise, the other anticlockwise, and as they did so the 'pattern' altered. Each layer could also move individually.

"Do you think there's a butterfly's wing hidden in there, like on your grandfather's desk?" Charley asked quietly, watching carefully as Luciana turned the box again, rotating another row of panels.

"There's not just one," she whispered. "There are four. One on each moving side of the box."

"How do you know that?"

"I remember playing with this when I was very small. I think it's one of the ways my grandfather tried to teach me to remember the wing patterns. See?" Luciana held it up, indicating its moving panels. "Every one of these can be rotated either left or right, and every time they are moved, the pattern on each side changes. There's a way to make all the wooden dots align in the right formations. I was never trying to do anything with the box when I was little – or at least, not at first. I just used to turn the tumblers. It was only later that Grandfather told me there were wing patterns hidden in there if I really looked closely. But I think this is a puzzle box too. If I can make all four wing decorations correctly at the same time, it will open – like the drawer in Grandfather's desk."

"But how on earth do you do that?" Charley asked, aghast. "Every time you move one side and get it right, the others will move too. How do you even know what wing you're trying to make?"

"That's why you have to know them all, I suppose," Luciana muttered, already absorbed by the box. "These were all butterflies that can be found in Great Britain, if I remember correctly. And I know them better than I did when I was little, so maybe…"

The light filtering down from the great glass roof began to fade as she kept turning the panels on the box, over and over, trying to get them to make patterns she recognized. Once she thought she had made a Red Admiral, but the last four tumblers would not connect properly and besides, there were no recognizable wings at all on the other three sides.

"Why do you think it was hidden in that place?" Charley asked at one point. "Do you think Adeline put it there when she went back?"

"Maybe," Luciana muttered. "Perhaps it was something my grandfather asked her to do."

"But why use one of your toys?"

Luciana shrugged and gave a quick grin. "Perhaps, like the puzzle on the desk, he wanted to know that only one person would know how it worked."

Luciana kept working on the box as the day dimmed even further. The library began to empty, and twice the librarian walked past their table, clearing his throat. Eventually Charley reached over the table and touched her arm.

"We must go back, Ana," he said softly. "If we don't get the next train we will be hopelessly late and there will be hell to pay as it is."

"Just another minute," she muttered. "Please. I'm almost there, if I can just…"

As she spoke Luciana turned a panel, but it still wasn't quite right – she had two wing patterns complete, but the other two were still missing part of their markings. She went back two steps, reversing what she had moved previously, and then moved two of the blocks in different directions before repeating the movement. There was a click. They stared at each other.

"Does … does that mean you did it?" Charley asked.

"I think so…" Luciana set the box down on the table. As soon as she let it go, the sliding panels all flipped outwards. A piece of paper popped out from within, fluttering down to land on the table between them.

Luciana reached out and picked it up.

"It's a name and address," she said. "For a Mr Philpot Danvers, of Richmond."

"That's all?" Charley asked.

"That's all."

Charley nodded. "Then I suppose we're not going home yet after all, are we?"

Chapter Twelve

The house stood beside the icy waters of the Thames. Luciana and Charley stood at its iron gate and stared along the darkened path. There were lights on behind drawn drapes, but the building lacked any aura of welcome. The renewed determination Luciana had felt after finding Danvers' name and address had begun to evaporate. Her feet were cold, the sleeves and shoulders of her wool coat were wet, and for the first time it had really occurred to her that they were stuck far from home in the middle of winter with nowhere to stay for the night. Luciana took a deep breath and gripped at the gate's handle before her resolve failed completely.

"Come on," she said. "We've come this far, haven't we?

We must at least knock."

"All right," Charley muttered, sounding no more sure than Luciana felt. "Let's give it a go then."

She pushed open the gate. They both winced as its hinges gave an abrupt squeal.

Halfway up the chequered path, Charley grabbed her arm. "I think we're being watched," he whispered, pointing to a large bay window to the right of the entranceway. The drapes were moving, as if someone had just dropped them back into place after looking out.

A moment later, the front door opened, emitting a glare of electric light. "Who's there?" demanded a strident male voice loudly. "I can see you lurking. Come into the light."

Luciana moved a step forward, Charley's hand still clamped firmly round her arm. Her eyes adjusted to the glare and she saw that the man at the door wore the crisp uniform of a butler. He looked them up and down.

"Who are you?" he said. "What do two ragamuffins want at this domicile? Be off with you!"

"We are looking for Mr Philpot Danvers," Luciana said, proud that her voice did not shake.

The butler's face remained impassive. "And why would you be looking for Mr Danvers?"

Luciana tried to work out what to say. It was too complicated to explain the whole truth.

"My grandfather sent me," she said.

The butler frowned. "And who, pray, is your grandfather?"

"His name was Marko Cattaneo. You might also have heard of him as the Magnificent Marko."

She saw the look on the butler's face change. Something flickered across it, disturbing his prim features.

"Come in," he said abruptly, opening the door wider.

Luciana and Charley looked at each other.

"Don't just stand there," said the servant. "I'm letting the night air in."

The two of them crossed the threshold into a hallway lined in dark, polished walnut. The butler led them into the room with the bay window, where a fire burned in an ornate iron grate.

"Wait," he ordered.

He disappeared again. Luciana looked around. The room was warm, thanks to the large fire. Instinctively she edged away from it, trying to pretend it wasn't there and turning to look at the two sofas upholstered in rich rose-pink silk instead. There was also a chaise longue set into the window bay along with a baby grand piano. A thick rug was on the floor, and the walls were crowded with paintings. The mantel over the fire held photographs and an elaborate brass clock.

"Not sure I like this," Charley muttered, eyeing the poker. "Be ready to make a run for it if we need to, all right?"

The door opened again, creaking on its hinges. Another man entered the room. He was thin and angular, with a thick shock of blond hair that dangled in unruly waves over his forehead. He swept it back as he entered to reveal eyes that were startlingly green and already crinkled by a smile. He pushed the door shut behind him and his shadow stretched up on to the ceiling. Everything about him seemed animated, as if he'd just been laughing at a joke. He was dressed in a fine suit of pale grey with a folded lilac kerchief in his top pocket.

"Well," he said in a loud, jovial voice. "What have we here then?"

"Are you … Mr Philpot Danvers?" Luciana asked hesitantly.

"I am indeed." Danvers strode towards her and bent a little at the waist to inspect her face. "And you're the Cattaneo, are you? Well, well. How on earth is the man himself? It's years since I've seen him. And what the blazes is he sending you to me for at this time of night?"

Luciana felt her optimism fading.

"My grandfather is dead," she said. "He died ten days ago."

At this news Danvers' jaw slackened and his skin seemed to take on a grey cast. He went to one of the sofas, sinking into it and gripping the arm with one hand. He stared at nothing for a moment, as if he'd forgotten that Luciana and Charley were even there.

"I'm sorry," he said with a voice as grey as his face. "I did not know. He … was ill?"

Luciana nodded, the sudden hot prick of tears taking her by surprise as she looked down at the carpet.

Danvers passed a hand over his face and then seemed to come to his senses a little. He looked up at them both and, realizing they were still standing, waved at them to sit before taking up a small bell on the table beside him and ringing it.

"Hot tea for us all, Turner, please," he said, when the man who had let them in appeared. "And find these two children something to eat, if you can."

Once the butler had vanished again, Danvers leaned forward, giving Luciana a serious look. "Your grandfather was a great man," he said. "I would have been at the funeral had I known. I've been abroad, you see. In America, as it happens. Only returned yesterday."

"How did you know my grandfather?" Luciana asked. "You were friends?"

Danvers nodded. "Yes, indeed. I love to travel, and as a

younger man your grandfather went all over the world. We had much in common, both in interests and the places we had both visited."

Luciana's heart sank further. She was becoming more and more convinced that Danvers would not be able to help them. He obviously saw her disappointment in her face.

"Why are you here, Luciana?" he asked. "What made you come to me?"

Luciana looked over at Charley, wondering how much to say. "We thought … we thought you'd be able to help us."

"With what, exactly?"

Luciana took a breath, looking at Charley again. Then she reached into the bag and drew out the velvet pouch, slipping the golden device from its innards. She laid it flat in her palm and held it out.

"We want to know what it is," Luciana said.

Danvers stared at it with no hint of recognition. "I have no earthly idea," he said, dashing the children's hopes once and for all. "I've never seen anything like it before, I'm afraid. What makes you think it's important?"

"It was hidden in my grandfather's study," Luciana explained.

"And this is what brought you to me?"

"Not exactly," Charley said. "It took us to the Peacock Theatre, and something we found *there* brought us here."

Danvers frown grew deeper. "Well then, what was that? Come on, my dears, I believe I have a right to know."

Luciana put her hand back into her bag and drew out the puzzle box they had found hidden behind the wardrobe. "This," she said.

Philpot Danvers blinked. "Aha," he said. "Well, now we're getting somewhere. I've got one of those too. Your grandfather gave it to me. It was one of the last times I saw him."

Chapter Thirteen

The puzzle box that Philpot Danvers brought to Luciana was different from the one she and Charley had found. Luciana looked at it in disappointment as Danvers handed it to her. When he'd said he was in possession of a box like hers, she'd envisioned another difficult time of trying to work out which wings were hidden amid the jumble, but she at least thought she'd know what she was doing. Danvers' box didn't seem to have anything similar at all. The pattern was just that – a pattern, made of circles set in long carved waves that covered all sides of the box. It was square, rather than oblong, and its surface was entirely flat. At first glance Luciana wasn't even sure it was a puzzle box at all.

"Oh, but it is," Danvers said, once she'd voiced this doubt. "Press one of the round inlays – the white circles. I think they're made of polished bone, or ivory, perhaps."

Luciana did as she was told and found that the circles depressed, like buttons. But beyond that, nothing at all seemed to happen.

"Well," said their host, as Turner came in with a tray laden with cold cuts of meat and slices of cake. "I could never get anywhere with it either. You can take it with you. Which reminds me – where are you both staying tonight? With some relative in town? Is that where Mrs Cattaneo is? I must say I'm rather surprised she hasn't accompanied you to my door. I would never have been allowed such freedom to roam when I was your age."

Charley and Luciana looked at each other. The guilt in their expressions must have given them away, because Danvers looked between them with a growing look of apprehension on his face.

"Good God. Please tell me that poor woman knows where you are?"

Luciana swallowed uncomfortably. "We thought we'd be able to get back home this evening and explain everything. But then we found the puzzle box – and then your name. We've missed the last train now."

"Do you mean she didn't even accompany you into

the city? But—" Danvers stopped, his face aghast. "Does that mean you don't have anywhere to stay tonight either?"

"We hadn't got that far yet," Charley admitted.

Danvers stood up abruptly and rang for Turner again. "I'm sorry for the late notice, Turner, but it seems we're going to need two extra beds turned down for the night."

The butler's stern gaze slid past his employer to the two children. "I believe I can facilitate that, sir."

"Thank you, my man. Oh, and I also need to send an urgent telegram out to the wilds of Sussex. Again, I know it's late, but…"

"I'll see to it, sir."

"Excellent. What would I do without you, Turner?"

The butler's expression suggested that such an eventuality would be a disaster of the sort that Danvers would not survive, but he said nothing, merely bowing once more before he departed.

"Come now," said Danvers. "Eat something, do. There's no standing on ceremony here, we're an informal household. The question is," he added, as Charley and Luciana both approached the table. "How am I going to entertain you both for the evening? I don't have much experience with children."

"You've already been very generous, Mr Danvers,"

Luciana said. "There's really no need to go to any more trouble."

"Nonsense," said the man, the animation that had been present when they had first seen him returning. "I bet you don't often get into town. Be a damned shame if you don't do something exciting while you're here. Thing is, I've been away for so long I don't know what the latest big thing is. Turner will though. He keeps his ear to the ground for me when I am away."

He rang the bell again and the butler appeared once more, looking a fraction more harried than he had the last time he had entered the room.

"Turner, my good, good man," Danvers said, his joviality now back in full force. "I am resolved to take these two young people to a show this evening. Might as well make the most of them being here, what? So – what have you been keeping note of for me?"

Turner's gaze flickered briefly to Luciana. "I am not sure what entertainments would be appropriate for a young lady to attend at this time of night, sir."

"Oh, tosh," Danvers said dismissively. "It's 1898, man. We're heading for a new millennium. Let's not have any of that stuffiness in this house. Come on – there must be something vital I've missed in my absence. What about magic? A magician would be perfect fare for the granddaughter of the Magnificent Marko, what?"

"There are very few magicians of note now, sir," said the butler. "The profession is rather fading away. In fact, I can think of only one in town at the moment. Adolphus Merritt. He has been playing at Weston's for the past two months."

Danvers brought his hands together with a resounding clap that made both Charley and Luciana jump. "Perfect! We should have time to make the evening performance!"

*

A little more than an hour later, Luciana and Charley found themselves following Philpot Danvers along a narrow row of seats in the already busy auditorium of Weston's Theatre.

"Don't you think this is all a bit odd?" Charley whispered to Luciana. "He's only just met us, he doesn't know us at all, and now he's putting us up and throwing money around to entertain us."

"He was a friend of my grandfather's, wasn't he?" Luciana pointed out, although she had to agree it was a little strange. "Let's not think about it now, all right? He's just being a gentleman."

"All right," Charley muttered. "If you say so."

Ahead of them, Danvers had drawn to a stop and was turning towards them. "Here we are," he called cheerfully, over the throng. "We're in this row. Not bad seats, eh?"

They said no more about it, but Charley's words niggled at Luciana. Still, they were here now, and as they settled themselves, Luciana looked around. It had been so long since she'd been in a theatre, and she felt an echo of the familiar excitement she'd always experienced as a child ringing in her heart. Weston's stage was shrouded from their view with a heavy curtain of midnight-blue velvet. Flickering stage lights lit the fabric in waves that rippled amid its folds. Then the orchestra struck up a merry tune and Luciana sat back to enjoy the show.

Chapter Fourteen

Adolphus Merritt was younger than Luciana had expected, dressed in a black coat and tails, and a long cloak lined with scarlet silk. He was not tall and walked with a cane, but he carried his back as straight as a ramrod. When he swept his top hat from his head, his thick dark hair was slicked back, except for an artful curl that had been shaped against his forehead. As the hat moved through the air, it produced a swarm of paper butterflies, their colours flickering in the dimmed stage light. The magician strode through the cloud of colour without even pausing to flourish at its appearance, or speak.

It soon became apparent that speaking was not a part of Adolphus Merritt's act. He uttered not a single word all the time he was on stage. At first Luciana found this strange, but soon she was so caught up in what was happening before her that she no longer noticed. It wasn't that Merritt was performing particularly spectacular tricks. Many of them were variations on illusions she had heard described by her grandfather over the years, or even seen him perform in his own show. Yet there was something mesmerizing about the figure on the stage – sometimes accompanied by an assistant, but more often performing before the crowd alone.

Either side of her, Luciana heard her own laughter and astonishment echoed by her companions. They were as entranced as the rest of the audience, entirely captivated by the movements of the magician on stage.

Still, despite her amazement, something else stole over Luciana as she watched. It was the sense that everything she saw before her was an elaborate artifice. At first she dismissed this simply because, after all, the audience was in the presence of a master illusionist. They had come to watch a man challenge reality in a way that made them shiver with amazement. The question she most heard murmured around her was 'How did he do that?'. They knew it wasn't 'real' magic. It just *looked* that way. But Luciana felt as if the magician himself was the illusion, as if she was watching someone wearing a mask. *That* was what Luciana found herself trying to peer behind.

For the finale, Merritt himself vanished in an explosion of sparks. The curtain came down and the audience got to their feet in a storm of furious clapping. Yet Merritt did not take a curtain call. Instead, as the thunder of applause rolled on and on, his assistant danced on from the wings, leaving in her wake a flurry of glitter. The audience were still on their feet when she stood on the thin lip in front of the fire curtain. She took a bow, then looked sharply up at the highest balcony to the left of the stage, just for a second. Luciana couldn't help but follow her glance, along with the rest of the audience. Out of the corner of her eye, Luciana saw the assistant raise one elegant arm and then – *BANG!* Another shower of sparks erupted in the place where she no longer stood.

The audience went into another paroxysm of clapping. Luciana, though, stood staring at the space that had just been occupied by Merritt's assistant. She stayed silent even as she followed Danvers and Charley through the jostling chaos of the departing audience and out into the cold February night.

"Well, what a show," Danvers declared as they stood waiting for their cab at the kerb outside the theatre. "Truly wonderful."

"I thought so too," Charley said, his face flushed pink and his eyes shining. "I think your grandfather would have loved it, don't you, Luciana?"

"Very much so." She smiled, though she could not remove the crease of a frown from her forehead.

"What's wrong?" Charley asked. "Didn't you think Merritt was brilliant? The way he never even said a word! And everything seemed so effortless, as if he were just floating through the world and things happened in his wake. Like that tree blooming and then producing oranges for his assistant to pick, right there on stage. Wasn't that extraordinary?"

"My grandfather used to do that too," Luciana said, and then admitted, "Although he didn't pick the oranges."

Their cab arrived and Danvers helped her in, peering at her face as they sat down. "Charley's right," he said. "Something about Merritt didn't sit well with you. What was it?"

"It's just ... there was something so strange about him, wasn't there? Didn't you feel it? As if we were watching someone putting on a face that wasn't really theirs."

"That's just part of the act, isn't it?" Charley asked. "Like the silence."

"Yes, yes," Danvers agreed. "It's all part of the show. And anyway, it may be that you are right, in a very literal sense. Many magicians take on a persona not their own. Perhaps, when Merritt is out and about during the day, he looks entirely different."

Luciana nodded absently. "And then there was his assistant," she said.

"She was very good," Danvers agreed. "I've seen a lot in my time and she's the only one who's come close to being as skilful as your grandfather's girl, Adeline Morrell."

"Did you know Adeline?" Charley asked. "We wanted to find her. Do you know where she went?"

"Ah, Adeline, poor girl. She couldn't get work here after the Marko debacle. She went abroad, I think. They do things differently there, you know."

"That's not what I was talking about," Luciana said. "I don't understand how they got away with it, if women aren't supposed to do magic."

"What do you mean?" asked Charley.

"At the end, when she came back on to do the curtain call," Luciana said. "She did the same vanishing trick that Merritt himself had done just moments before."

"Oh, she didn't do that." Danvers laughed. "Merritt was up there on the balcony, directing the trick from above."

"Was he?" Luciana asked. "Did you see him?"

"I – well, no, I didn't," Danvers admitted. "Not exactly.

But he was there – the whole audience looked up and saw him."

"Did they?" Luciana asked doubtfully.

"Why yes, of course." Danvers laughed again. "It was the one time she slipped up in the whole performance, actually. I thought it even at the time. *She'll have hell to pay after the show*, I thought. I bet she's getting a ticking-off at this moment, in fact. She glanced right up at him just a second or two before he performed the trick. Didn't you see?"

"I saw her look up," said Luciana. "The whole audience saw her look up. But I didn't see Merritt on the balcony. Did you, Charley?"

"No, I didn't," Charley admitted.

"That's because he wasn't there," said Luciana. "She just made everyone think that he was before she did the trick herself and disappeared. The look up at the balcony was just misdirection, to make everyone think she was checking for Merritt. Then she did the trick herself."

Danvers laughed heartily. "Oh, poppycock," he said. "It was Merritt all right. Of course it was. Ask a hundred people in the audience tonight and they'll all say they saw him up there – because he must have been there. There's no other explanation."

Luciana said nothing more as they rattled over the cobbled streets, back towards Philpot Danvers' house.

She knew what she'd seen and what she hadn't seen because it hadn't been there. They hadn't needed magic to pull the biggest trick that had been performed that evening. They'd just needed misdirection.

It's the greatest trick a magician has.

Luciana looked out at the gaslit streets. Adolphus Merritt was the big new thing on the London stage. Anyone who was anyone must have been to see his performance, and that surely included Carl Thursby. Why hadn't Merritt suffered the same fate as her grandfather? Because as far as she could see, he'd been teaching his assistant in just the same way, and to Luciana that just wasn't fair. The injustice of it seemed insurmountable. Her anger grew so that by the time they had reached Philpot Danvers' house, it was a towering inferno that consumed her.

Refusing their new friend's offer of a late supper, Luciana said a quick goodnight and went up to the bedroom that had been prepared for her. It was at the side of the house, in a funny little turret attached to the eaves. Luciana, too agitated to sleep, was drawn instead to the window. It was set in an alcove, low enough that she could kneel on the floor and lean on the sill. One side of it looked out over the Thames, glinting now in the light of a moon that had forced its way through a thick layer of cloud. Luciana watched the tumble and trip of the water, her thoughts as agitated as the river below. She thought of Danvers' puzzle box. *I'm too angry to sleep*, she thought. *I might as well do* something *useful.*

Luciana got up, went to her bag and took out the box, returning to the window again to sit down and study it properly.

Chapter Fifteen

Breakfast the next morning was taken in a room looking out over a garden full of unmarked snow. Luciana and Charley sat at the table, waiting for Philpot to join them. The puzzle box was between them, still firmly closed.

"Don't feel bad that you couldn't open it," Charley told her. "Maybe Philpot will let you take it with you when we go home so that you can carry on trying. He did say he would, didn't he?"

Luciana said nothing, just helped herself to some toast and strawberry jam. Turner was pouring her a cup of tea when the door opened.

"Well, well, well!" Danvers exclaimed, entering the room like a hurricane. "What a wonderful day it is, to come downstairs from a good night's sleep to find two such marvellous guests at breakfast!"

Luciana and Charley both mumbled good mornings as he filled a plate from the buffet table. Turner picked up a small silver tray bearing a white envelope and proffered it to his employer.

"Aha," Danvers said. "A telegram. An answer to mine of yesterday from your poor families, no doubt."

He read the telegram briefly and sighed, then passed it over for Luciana to see.

Sincere thanks for your kindly intervention *stop* **Please return children by earliest available train** *stop* **Will reimburse** *stop* **Best wishes** *stop* **I Cattaneo** *stop*

"Short and to the point," Danvers said cheerfully. "But that means that's the end of that, I'm afraid. Your London adventure must end here. I am duty bound to do as your grandmother says."

He sat down at the head of the table and noticed the puzzle box for the first time. "No luck, eh, Luciana dear?" he asked. "Ah well, never mind. Some mysteries are meant to stay unsolved, eh? You must take it with you, as a gift."

"Oh no," said Luciana. "The box was a present to you, not me. You must keep it and open it yourself."

She felt Charley's eyes on her, but avoided his gaze. Sometimes he knew her just a little too well.

"True, very true," Danvers said. "Well, if you are sure, then here it shall stay, my dear. I shall certainly keep at it. Yes, I certainly will. Come now, eat up. We must away to the station. I do believe there is a train departing for Rotherton in less than an hour."

After breakfast Luciana retrieved her bag and said goodbye to the little bedroom. From one of the windows she could see Turner at the kerb, standing beside a cab. One of the horses stamped and whickered impatiently.

"Thank you, Mr Danvers," Luciana said, as she came back down and met him and Charley in the hallway. "We are so grateful for your hospitality."

"Oh, pish," said Philpot. "It has been my absolute pleasure. I am sorry it has been such a short visit, and that you did not find what you were looking for. But we do not need to say our goodbyes yet. I shall accompany you to the station."

"Oh no, really, there's no need." Luciana smiled. "I am sure you must have many affairs of your own to take care of."

"But I must see you safe home," Danvers said. "Or at least, as far as I can take you personally, which in this case means putting you on that train."

Luciana felt Charley's eyes on her again. "You are putting us in a cab directly there, Mr Danvers. I assure you, we will be quite safe. And really, we have trespassed upon your generosity so much already."

Philpot Danvers rubbed his chin. "As it happens I do have a meeting with a chap later. But I can still do both…"

"Really, there's no need," Luciana insisted. "You've already done more than enough."

Danvers sighed. "All right. Well, I don't mind telling you, it would be rather useful, today of all days. Turner," he called, raising his voice. "Please give the money for train tickets to Miss Cattaneo. They are going to see themselves to the train." He looked down at Luciana again. "Just be sure to let me know when you reach home, won't you?"

"We will. And thank you again, Mr Danvers," Luciana said. "You really have been most kind."

"All right," Charley said, as the carriage pulled away. "What's going on? And why do I have a horrible feeling that we're not getting on a train home?"

"We will," Luciana promised. "But we can't go straight back. We need to go somewhere else first."

"Where?"

"To a place called the Brown Bear in Whitechapel." Luciana reached into her pocket and held up a slip of paper. "And before you ask what's there, I don't know. But that's the address that was written on this piece of paper that was inside Philpot Danvers' puzzle box."

Charley shook his head. "I knew it. You *did* manage to open it! Why didn't you want Danvers to know?"

Luciana shrugged. "I don't trust him. I liked him at first, but like you said, something just doesn't feel right. If he was such a close friend of my grandfather's, why did he never visit us in Midford? And if he was meant to have the puzzle box, wouldn't my grandfather have given him one with a key that was something he knew about?"

"What was the key, anyway?" Charley asked.

"It was the complete wing pattern of a female Swallowtail," Luciana said. "It was spread over all six sides of the box, so I had to think of it in sections. I don't think Mr Philpot Danvers is ever likely to work that out, do you?"

Chapter Sixteen

It took them an hour to reach the Brown Bear after asking directions from an off-duty guard at Charing Cross. The route they had been pointed towards took them along the curving edge of the Thames. The tide was out and so they walked on the river's icy shore, stepping over slippery driftwood and on the crushed shells of oysters thrown from the balconies of the wharfs and taverns above. They came up from the shoreline to pass over the narrow bridge at the busy entrance of St Katherine Docks. At Wapping High Street, they turned inland, along busy streets thronged with hawkers and lined with slush. They passed a music hall called Wilton's, closed since it wasn't yet even midday. Then, a little further on, there was the Brown Bear public house. It occupied the ground floor of a three-storey building of sand-coloured brick, with an archway to its right that led to a coaching courtyard behind.

Luciana looked up at the building, suddenly apprehensive about what they may find inside. She'd never been inside a pub before. But then, she reflected, she'd never done a lot of the things that she'd done over the past couple of days, and so far everything had turned out fine.

"Come on," she said to Charley. "Let's get on with it."

Inside, the pub was dingy, uncertain light falling from the oil lamps set in the wall and through the grubby windows. One long bar of dark wood ran along the middle of the narrow space, with tables and chairs dotted around the wooden floor. Luciana led the way. A large man in a greasy shirt was behind the bar. He leaned on it heavily as they approached.

"Well, well," he said, looking them up and down. "What have we here then?"

"Just two hungry travellers looking for a meal," Luciana said, sounding bolder than she felt.

The man looked amused. "And a little chit to speak for them both," he said. "Well, we don't hold nothing against the different in here. We've got oysters and bacon with good beer gravy. I'll send over a couple of platefuls."

Charley led the way to an unoccupied table beneath

one of the windows.

"So," he said. "Do you think this is the place, or not?"

"It must be," Luciana said. "It's definitely the place that was hidden inside the puzzle. But I don't know what we're supposed to be looking for."

Charley stood up. "I'm going to take a look around," he said. "I'll be back."

He walked past one end of the bar, as if he were heading for the conveniences or the kitchen, all situated at the back of the room. Then he turned left and vanished from view along a passageway that ran behind the bar. He reappeared at the other end a couple of minutes later and beckoned to Luciana, who got up and hurried over.

"Look," he said, pointing to one of the posters on the drab wall. It hung in an ornate wooden frame, its colours an unexpected rainbow in the dimness of the passageway.

The Magnificent Marko!

Be Amazed!

Be Entranced!

Be Flabbergasted!

Behold the Most Extraordinary Sights ever seen on the London Stage!

"That's one of Grandfather's posters!" Luciana exclaimed. "But what's it doing here?"

Behind them the door to what was evidently the kitchen

swung open in a flurry of greasy smells. The barkeep appeared, bearing two steaming plates of food.

"What're you two doing back here?" he asked. "I've got your grub. You'll want it while it's hot."

Charley pointed at the poster. "Why have you got that?" he asked.

The barkeep glanced at it and gave a short grunt. Then he turned his head back to the kitchen door raised his voice in a shout.

"Fervent!" he bellowed. "You're wanted!"

Chapter Seventeen

Timothy Fervent was a small plump man with a salutation of red hair and very anxious eyes.

"I cannot believe it," he murmured in an accent that drifted over the sea from Ireland. "That you should find me here. How did you know where I was?"

"I didn't, but –" Luciana took out the piece of paper that had been folded inside the puzzle box – "my grandfather sent me here. Well, in a manner of speaking, I think he did, anyway."

"The question is," Fervent asked, "why did your grandfather want anyone to find me at all? I'm a cook in a pub, and before that I was just a barkeep in another pub. I'm not important."

"Is that how you knew Marko?" Charley asked.

"Yes." Fervent sighed. "He used to come into the last place I worked. That was up on the Charing Cross Road. We got to talking one day and then it happened that we got to be friends. I even came to see the show one night. He got me front-row tickets. Right proud to be there, I was. It was the only night that he ever performed the Golden Butterfly. I was one of the first to see it, and the last." The man shook his head. "A terrible shame, all that business."

"Did he talk to you about it?" Charley asked around a final mouthful of oysters and bacon. "What happened with Thursby and the Grand Society of Magicians, I mean?"

At the mention of Thursby's name, Fervent's eyes turned baleful. "That devil. No, Marko never spoke of it, save when he told me he'd not be in any more. That was only a week or so after that show, and Thursby was hounding him even then. He followed your grandfather in and sat watching us as if we were criminals. Then he got up and went without even buying a drink. He left two of his lackeys in the bar instead. They came in every day for two weeks after that, just to stare at me. That's why I quit and came here. Felt as if I were under siege. And for what? As if a great man like that would tell someone like me any secrets. They just enjoyed the bullying, if you ask me. Small men with small lives given a sense of power –

they're by far the worst kind of men to walk this earth."

Luciana pushed her plate aside. "What about that poster on the wall back there," she asked. "Where did that come from?"

"Ah, well," said Fervent. "It turned up here about a week after I started this job. There weren't a note or anything with it, and Lord only knows how your grandfather knew where I was. It's not as if there aren't pubs aplenty in London town, and I didn't tell him where I was going. It must have come from him though, mustn't it? I took it as a little thank-you for all our chats. T'aint nowhere for me to hang it in the eaves of the attic where I bed down and it's too fine not to be seen, so I asked if I could hang it here."

"It arrived as it is now?" Charley asked. "In that frame?"

"Why, yes, for which I was doubly grateful," said Timothy Fervent. "It is a very fine frame indeed. Like nothing I could have afforded myself."

Luciana and Charley looked at each other across the table.

"Would you … permit me to examine it?" Luciana asked. "Could we remove it from the wall?"

"I don't see why not."

"I can see why not," the barkeep barked across the room. "You're supposed to be out the back slaving over a hot stove, not having a chinwag."

"Let me just get it down for them," said the cook, standing up. "Then I'll get back in the kitchen."

Fervent disappeared into the passage, reappearing a couple of minutes later hefting the poster in its frame. Charley hastily moved their empty plates out of the way so that he could lay it down on the table in front of them.

"All right," Fervent said. "I don't know what earthly good it'll do you, but you take a look. I'll be back as soon as I can."

With that, he returned to the kitchen. A moment later the sound of whooshing steam and clanging pans echoed from the back of the pub. Luciana began to examine the frame. The decoration was ornate; deep curlicues and whorls in a baroque pattern that was nothing like the oriental style of her grandfather's desk or the boxes she'd deciphered.

"I don't think this is going to help us," she said after a while. "I think it's just what it looks like – a picture in a frame."

"Let's not give up yet," Charley said. "Turn it over and we'll have a look at the back."

Together they flipped the frame over so that the poster was lying face down on the table, but the board this revealed was smooth and featureless. It seemed impossible that such a blank surface could hold any secrets at all.

"Well," Charley said gloomily, after another thorough examination had yielded no clues. "Maybe you're right and this was nothing but a wild goose chase after all."

"What's that?" Fervent asked, appearing back at the table.

"It's just the back of the frame," Luciana told him, "and there's nothing on it to help us at all."

"No," said the cook, pointing at the edge of the frame. "I meant *those*."

Luciana and Charley leaned over to see what he was pointing at. There, set in the edge of the frame, was a short line of what looked like tiny gold rivets.

"That's odd," said Charley, examining the rest of the frame. "There aren't any more elsewhere. I don't think they're to hold the frame together."

Luciana ran a thumbnail across the wood surrounding the rivets. It felt slightly uneven. "I think there's a join in the wood," she said. "Maybe a drawer?"

"If it is, it's no deeper than a Penny Dreadful is thick," said Fervent. "What good is anything inside it going to be?"

"Well, let's find out," Luciana said. She reached up to her hair and took out one of the pins holding some of her curls in place. Then she pulled the pin apart until it was

just a very slim, straight piece of metal. She fitted one end
to the head of the last rivet in the row and pushed. It gave,
just a little.

Chapter Eighteen

Fervent glanced over his shoulder at the bar as Luciana was pushing her hairpin into the final rivet. The pub had begun to fill since they'd sat down, and the barkeep was occupied with too many customers to notice that he wasn't in the kitchen.

Luciana pushed the final rivet back and almost immediately a narrow panel popped open. Rather than a drawer, it was simply a thin flap of wood, no more than half a centimetre wide and the length of the hairpin she'd used to open it. Peering inside, Luciana could see something lodged in the space within.

"What is it?" Thomas asked, leaning in.

"I don't know…" Luciana tried to lift the frame to tip

whatever it was out, but it wouldn't budge. "It's stuck."

"Use the hairpin again," Charley suggested. "Maybe you can coax it out?"

Luciana bent the pin back against itself to form a sort of 'L' shape and tried to hook it around the object in the frame. The pin kept giving way, and she had to keep pulling it out and straightening the two arms of the 'L' before trying again.

"It's moving," she said, teeth gritted. "I think—"

At that moment a tiny gleam of gold appeared, as whatever it was reached the edge of the frame. Luciana grasped it with her fingertips. Bit by bit, the sliver of metal grew larger and larger. Luciana looked up at Charley.

"I know what it is," she said.

"Yeah," said Charley, "I think I do too."

One final tug and there it lay on the table, strangely wing-shaped, with a tiny rivet in each corner.

"Well," said Fervent, leaning back with a perplexed look on his face. "I'm glad you two know what it is, because I haven't got a clue. And I don't think it's real gold neither."

Luciana was already fumbling in her bag. "It's not," she said. "We think it's made of brass. Like this one."

She pulled out what she'd been seeking and laid it on the table. The two devices – the one she'd found in her grandfather's desk and the one she had just succeeded in freeing – were almost identical. There was just one difference. The second device had no ribbon-thin piece of metal leading from it – although it did have a tiny scar where, perhaps, such a thing had once been joined.

"Well," said Charley. "Would you look at that?"

He reached out and rearranged the two pieces so that they lay side by side, close enough that the ribbon of metal leading from the first touched the scar on the second.

Luciana and Charley looked at each other across the table. "What does that look like to you?" she asked.

Charley grinned. "It looks like a pair of wings. *Butterfly* wings. Golden ones!"

Luciana stared down at the two pieces. "Is this what Thursby is looking for?" she whispered. "Is this what he's been trying to find for so long?"

"It's got to be, hasn't it?" Charley said.

"So … this is the secret to making the trick work then?" she asked. "But … how?" She peered into the gap left in the frame but it was empty. "There aren't any instructions and we already know we couldn't work out what was inside."

Charley shrugged. "Perhaps we needed both pieces?"

Luciana rubbed a hand over her face and sighed. "What we need is someone who can tell us what exactly it is and how it works."

Timothy Fervent reached out and covered both pieces with his hand, pushing them back towards Luciana. "Well, until you find that person, better keep them both under wraps," he said, glancing over her head and scanning the crowd that had filled the room around them. "Never know who's watching, do you?"

Luciana opened her bag and slipped the two small golden wings into it. "What are we going to do now?"

Charley looked at the time on the large clock that hung behind the bar. "We need to start making our way back to the station if we're going to get back to Rotherton tonight."

"We can't stop now," Luciana protested. "We still don't know what the golden wings do!"

"We don't even know who to ask for help in working that out," Charley pointed out.

Fervent glanced over to the bar again and leaned in. "If it makes any difference, I think I know who you need to be looking for." He nodded at Luciana's bag. "If anyone's going to know what to do with that thing you've got there, it'll be Adeline."

"Adeline?" Luciana repeated. "You mean ... Adeline Morrell? My grandfather's assistant?"

Fervent nodded. "I bet she'd be able to help you, if you can find her."

"But she's not in England any more, is she?" Charley

asked. "When the Magnificent Marko quit the stage, didn't she go abroad? That's what Philpot Danvers told us."

Timothy Fervent frowned. "Philpot Danvers?"

"Do you know him?" Luciana asked. "He was a friend of my grandfather's too."

"Was he?" Fervent asked. "Are you sure?"

Luciana and Charley looked at each other with a frown. "Well, he said he was," she said. "One of the clues we found sent us to him. And he had one of my grandfather's puzzle boxes – the one that led us here. Why?"

Fervent glanced towards the bar again. The crowd had thinned a little. "You remember I told you that Carl Thursby had two men watching your grandfather and me? One of them was Philpot Danvers."

"What?" said Charley, shocked.

"That's not all," said Fervent, leaning closer still. "The other man … is standing at the bar this very moment."

Luciana looked over her shoulder, searching the sea of faces for someone she recognized. One in particular caught her eye. It was a man with a cloth cap pulled down low over his eyes. He was leaning on the bar, holding a pint of beer in one hand. There was a newspaper beside him and he looked as if he were reading it. But as Luciana watched, she saw him glance in their direction. His eyes met Luciana's. She turned away sharply.

"It's Turner," she said hoarsely. "It's Danvers' butler! He must have followed us! Do you think he saw the golden wings?"

Fervent shook his head. "I don't think so. He wasn't at the bar when I came out of the kitchen. He must have been outside, waiting for a crowd to come in so he could slip by unnoticed."

"What are we going to do?" Charley asked. "If he and Danvers are spies for Thursby…"

"Is there a back way out of here?" Luciana asked Fervent.

Fervent shrugged. "There's the kitchen entrance. It leads to the stable courtyard. But if you both follow me into the kitchen what's-his-name over there will know something's afoot."

"We'll have to split up," Luciana decided. "Timothy, you go back to the kitchen. In a few minutes I'll pretend to get up to powder my nose but come into the kitchen instead. Charley, you go out the front. Turner will have to decide who to follow. While he's deciding, we can get away."

"And go where?" Charley asked. "Please say we're going back to the station. Please say we're going home."

Luciana pressed her lips together. "Let's talk about that once we're out of here, shall we?" She looked at Fervent. "When you're ready."

Timothy Fervent nodded. He leaned back in his chair, looked at his watch and tapped it once. "Better be getting back to the pots and pans," he said.

Then he got up and walked away.

Chapter Nineteen

"Run," Luciana hissed, when she saw Charley waiting for her a little way down the street. "*Run!*"

Luciana glanced behind her to see if Turner was following as they fled, but couldn't see him. Eventually they found themselves in a narrow alleyway that led down to the river and stopped to catch their breath.

"Right," said Charley, once he could speak again. "Let's head back to the station."

"We can't go back now!" Luciana said. "If we do it'll all be over. Danvers and Turner are spies for Thursby, and I showed one of the wings to Danvers, so Thursby will soon know that we've found the Golden Butterfly, if he doesn't know already! If Thursby turns up at the house again…"

"I thought you said your grandmother told him he'd never be let back in after last time?" Charley asked. "Anyway, you could hide both in the desk. They'd never find them there."

"They would," Luciana cried, "I told Danvers that we'd found the first piece in Grandfather's study, didn't I? He'll tear it apart to find the Golden Butterfly! I can't go back. Not yet. If they find it now it'll be all my fault! You go home. Tell my grandmother I'm all right. I'll find somewhere to stay tonight. I could go back to the Peacock Theatre. I'm sure Mr Hibberd would let me sleep in Grandfather's old dressing room."

Charley stared at her. "What kind of friend would leave you here alone? If you won't come home, I'm going to have to stay too. And if I'm going to stay, then there had better be a pretty good reason for me making my mother worry. So we'd better come up with a plan. All right?"

Luciana bit her lip and looked at him. "I do have a plan. Sort of. What we need is someone to tell us what these devices are. Right?"

"I thought we'd decided the person to do that was Adeline Morrell? We don't know where she is."

"No, we don't," Luciana agreed. "But my grandfather must have had a reason to hide them so well. He must have thought that someone else could work out how to

138

use them if they were found, otherwise he wouldn't have bothered, would he?"

"That makes sense," said Charley.

"Right. So we need another magician. One we can trust not to just hand us and the devices over to Thursby."

"But we don't know any other magicians!"

"We've seen one though, haven't we? A really good one too. Adolphus Merritt."

Charley frowned. "Why would he help us? He doesn't know us. We've never even met him."

Luciana shouldered her cloth bag with a small but triumphant smile. "Because I noticed something that night that no one else did."

*

Weston's stage door was large and black with shining paint that looked quite new. Charley pulled the bell-rope that hung beside it and they waited, listening to the hubbub from the street.

"We're here to see Adolphus Merritt's assistant," Luciana told the boy who opened the door.

"No visitors before the performance," said the child smartly, pushing the door shut again.

Luciana put the toe of her boot in the gap before it could close. "She'll make an exception for me," she said quietly. "Go and tell her that someone's looking for the woman who can do magic as well as her master. I want to talk to her. Before I talk to ... anyone *else*."

The boy gave her a blank look, but also added a curt nod. "Clara," he said. "That's who you mean. I'll get her."

Luciana removed her foot and he shut the door. They listened to his footsteps echo away into the depths of the theatre.

"What are you up to?" Charley asked Luciana, suspiciously. "What was all that about?"

Luciana turned to him. "I told you I had a plan. This is it."

"I'm not convinced it's a very good one," Charley muttered, as they heard two pairs of swift footsteps echoing back towards them.

The stage door was flung open again to reveal the young woman whom Luciana had first seen on stage just last night. She was dressed in a long kimono with a pattern of bright red flowers over black silk. Her dark hair was down around her shoulders and she was clearly furious. The boy lurked behind her.

"Ben, go back to your duties," Clara told him, and then waited until he'd gone. Then she turned to Luciana and Charley. "Now, what the devil do you two want?"

140

"Your help," Luciana told her. "That's all. We just want your help."

The woman crossed her arms. "And you think the best way of getting it is by threatening me, do you? You've got a grand cheek. Be off with you, before I scream for the police."

"If you do that, I'll go to Thursby," Luciana said, steeling herself. "I swear I will."

A flicker of something like fear passed through the woman's eyes, though it was quickly replaced by a glare as hard as flint.

"And what makes you think the master of the Grand Society of Magicians will listen to a word you have to say?"

"Because I know you performed that trick yourself, right in front of an entire audience," Luciana said. "And even if he doesn't want to believe it, he'll watch the show to be sure. He'll be waiting for it and he'll see you do it, just like I did. Then where will you – and Adolphus Merritt – be?"

Clara sucked an angry breath through her gritted teeth before pulling the door open wider. "You've got five minutes and not a second beyond. I've got things to do."

They followed her along the echoing corridor to her dressing room.

"Women can't do magic," Clara said, once the door was shut behind them.

"Yes, they can," Luciana countered. "They're just not supposed to. That's not the same thing. Is it?"

The hard glint in the woman's eye became something else. For a second Luciana thought she might even smile, but it was gone in an instant. "Who are you?"

"My name is Luciana. Luciana Cattaneo. This is my friend, Charley. My grandfather was the Magnificent Marko."

At Luciana's announcement the woman's face changed completely. Instead of anger, outright panic flashed across her face. She dropped her arms, her mouth slightly agape.

"What are *you* doing *here*? How did you find us? Who told you?"

"I – we came to see the performance last night," Luciana said, confused. "We need someone who knows magic to help us, someone who won't go straight to Thursby when we show them—"

Luciana's words were drowned out by a knock at the door that was sharp enough to make them all jump, but Clara most of all. She stepped swiftly to the door and opened it just a crack.

"You don't need to be here," she said in an urgent whisper to the person beyond. "I can deal with this. Stay away."

The door was pushed open anyway. The heavy tap of a walking cane thumped against the bare floorboards as the person walked into the room.

Luciana found herself looking into the clear, calm eyes of Adolphus Merritt.

Chapter Twenty

The magician stood over Luciana and Charley with a face as still as ice. Up close, Luciana still had the sense that she was only seeing an illusion, rather than the truth of the person standing in front of her. Merritt looked her over from head to foot, but Luciana refused to shrink back. Here was a magician who had done exactly the same as her grandfather, but had avoided the punishment that had ended the Magnificent Marko's career. Why should she be the one to be afraid?

"I can deal with this," Clara said to Merritt. "You should go."

Merritt gave a single shake of his head and then moved to sit in the armchair that stood beside the small fireplace.

Once settled, he looked at Clara again, raising one eyebrow.

Clara cleared her throat. "Say it again. Who you are, I mean."

Luciana glanced at Merritt in surprise. She'd assumed that the magician's silence was just for the stage. Could it really be true that he never spoke at all?

"My name is Luciana Cattaneo. My grandfather was—" Luciana faltered at the reaction the simple recitation of her name had provoked in the magician. His eyes, wide now, flashed to hers and then roved over her face for a second. Then, just as abruptly, he turned away again. "My – my grandfather was the Magnificent Marko. He died almost two weeks ago."

"I'm sorry about that, but what do you want here?" Clara asked, her voice rough. "What do you want from us?"

Luciana shifted from one foot to the other. "Carl Thursby brought men to our house on the day of my grandfather's funeral. They were searching for something. It was his last trick. The one that got him banished from the stage because he taught it to his assistant, Adeline Morrell. The Golden Butterfly."

Luciana saw Merritt's shoulders stiffen, but he otherwise showed no sign that he was even listening.

"We found it," Luciana went on. "What my grandfather had hidden from Thursby. We think it's the key to the

Golden Butterfly, but we don't know how it works. We need someone who knows magic properly to help us. We need a magician."

"None of this has anything to do with us," Clara said a little desperately.

"I know it doesn't," said Luciana. "And I promise, I don't mean you any harm. All I want is some answers."

"But you threatened us," the woman hissed. "What makes you think we would trust you?"

"Why *should* you be able to trust me?" Luciana asked, becoming angry herself. "I saw you do that trick. I saw you! How is what Merritt has taught you any different than what my grandfather taught his own assistant? And yet no one is hounding you. Thursby hasn't had you thrown off the stage, made you give up your livelihood, what you love, had your friends followed and spied upon! My grandfather lost everything, and here you are, doing exactly as you please and not a word said. How is that fair?"

Merritt turned his head at that. He and Clara shared a long, silent look.

"What is it that you want to know?" Clara asked eventually, turning to Luciana.

Luciana looked at Charley. "Before I show you, you have to promise. You have to promise not to tell Thursby we have it."

Clara made a sound in her throat and shook her head. "Believe me, whatever it is, neither of us have any interest in doing that."

Luciana paused another moment.

"Come on, Ana," Charley said. "It's now or never, isn't it? Where else are we going to go?"

Luciana reached into her bag and took out the pouch. Opening it, she tipped both gold pieces into her hand and held them out to Clara. Merritt's assistant took them and examined them with a frown before handing them to the magician.

Adolphus Merritt held a golden wing in each hand, smoothing his thumbs across the polished brass. He bent over them in silent contemplation for a few moments and then shook his head. Turning back to Luciana he held the two pieces out to her.

"What does that mean?" Luciana asked, not taking them from him. "That you can't help us? Or that you won't?"

The magician ran one thumb across the severed end of the metal ribbon that once connected the two pieces, and shrugged.

"It's broken," Luciana said, frustrated. "I can see that. But what does it do? How does it work? What—"

Merritt stood up from the chair and approached her. Taking one of Luciana's hands he put both pieces into it

147

and wrapped her fingers over it. He smiled down at her, and for a moment the clear blue of his eyes transformed into the warm brilliance of a summer sky. Luciana stared in shock as something in her mind flared in recognition. She knew those eyes. She *remembered* them, from long ago. But she'd never been this close to Merritt before. Had she?

"We can't help you," said Clara. "So you'll have to decide what to do. If you want to go to Thursby, we can't stop you."

Luciana looked at her. "What would be the good of that?" she asked. "You'll just change the act."

Clara shrugged, her face hard. "Well then," she said. "Either way you've stopped us, haven't you?"

Luciana looked down at the pieces of metal in her hand. "I just want to know what this is. I want to know why it's so important to Thursby."

"Why?" Clara asked, exasperated. "What good would that do?"

Luciana blinked, tears in her eyes. "I never knew my parents. My grandparents are all I had. Now my grandfather is gone too. This is all I have left of him, but I don't even really understand what it is. He left both of these pieces somewhere that he knew only I could find them. I feel as if he wanted me to work this out, to follow this trail, but this is where it has led me, and I still don't understand. My grandmother wants me to forget all about magic completely, now that the Magnificent Marko has gone. But I don't want to forget him, or what he did, or how great his magic was. The world might be forgetting the Magnificent Marko – they might be forgetting magic altogether – but I don't want to. I want to understand it. I want to know how to perform it, and then maybe…" she trailed off, her shoulders sagging, feeling defeated, not even sure, really, what it was she was trying to express. After all, what could one girl do against a whole world of forgetting?

Charley took her hand. "Come on," he said quietly. "There's no point staying here. Let's go."

Luciana let him pull her away, the two pieces of broken trick in her hand. Neither Clara nor Adolphus Merritt tried to stop them.

"I'm sorry," Clara called after them. "I'm sorry that we can't help you."

At the door Luciana looked back. Merritt was watching her, a sad smile frozen on his pale face, and there was something about it that stabbed a knife through Luciana's heart. It was an expression that was familiar and at the same time like nothing she had ever seen before.

Something appeared from the muddled gloom of her own mind – another flash of memory, as powerful as the fragment that had accosted her in the dressing room at the Peacock.

She was wrapped in a soft blanket, warm and sleepy. Someone was singing to her. There was a face too. Bright blue eyes and a smile—

Luciana gasped and staggered, bracing herself against the doorjamb as Charley reached out to steady her.

"What is it?" he said, alarmed. "What's wrong?"

Luciana stared past him, straight at the magician, who was watching her carefully. "I know," she said. "I know why Adolphus Merritt never speaks. He doesn't exist, does he? He never has. You're not Adolphus Merritt. You're Adeline Morrell."

Chapter Twenty-one

There was a moment of absolute silence. Then Clara gave a high laugh.

"That's the most absurd thing I've ever heard! How completely ridiculous!"

"No, it's not," said Luciana. She kept her eyes on the magician, who was standing in silence, still watching her. "Magicians use disguises all the time. Philpot Danvers even said so, when we came to see you perform. They use them as part of their act. Some even go as far as living their whole lives behind a mask to make their performances work. That's what you've done, isn't it? Except your deception is even greater than that. You've made everyone believe you are a man called Adolphus Merritt. But you're not. You're a woman. A woman called Adeline Morrell."

Clara laughed again, a short, desperate sound. "Oh, enough of this. Go on, get out of here. We've got a show to prepare!"

"I'm not leaving," Luciana said. "You'll have to carry me out and throw me into the street if you want to get rid of me. Because I know I'm right. Aren't I?"

There was another moment of silence. Then Merritt spoke.

"What gave me away?"

It was clearly a woman's voice. Luciana blinked in surprise even though she'd been expecting it. Behind her, she heard Charley gasp. Luciana studied the magician's face. "The eyes," she said. "And the mouth. I recognized you the first moment I saw you on stage, I just didn't know why. It's your nose, isn't it? It's fake. That's where the mask is."

Merritt sighed. Then he reached up and ran the fingers of one hand down his nose. He grasped it and yanked, hard. Clara gasped out a "No!" as it came away.

"There," said Adeline Morrell, holding up the ruin of rubber for Luciana and Charley to see before tossing it to the floor.

"Adeline, what have you done?" Clara cried, darting for the door and leaning hard against it, as if to be sure no one else could come in and see Merritt's unveiling. "Why didn't you just send them away? Now we are finished!"

"Oh, Clara," said Adeline Morrell. "The game is up. There's no point pretending otherwise. It was up the moment Luciana knocked at our door." Morrell looked at Luciana with a sad smile. "Well, well. Now you know the truth, and I am sure you must have questions."

"Yeah," said Charley, finding his voice. He waved his hand at Morrell's black suit and tails. "I've got one. *Why?*"

Adeline put her hands on her hips and laughed. "A question only a lad could ask." She looked at Luciana. "I'll let you answer that one, my dear."

"Because women aren't allowed to do magic," Luciana said quietly. "They're only allowed to be assistants."

"Exactly right." Morrell looked down at herself. "And to be honest, a sharp suit has always seemed far more stylish to me than a corset and a cumbersome gown. It's so much easier to move in, for one thing. But I could never get the voice right, so I decided to forego it entirely."

"There's the eyes too," said Luciana. "You couldn't hide your eyes. How did no one else recognize them?"

Morrell was amused. "It is a truth universally acknowledged, my child, that men rarely pay much attention to a woman's eyes. Besides, no one ever really notices the assistant. They're dazzled by how pretty she is, but they

153

don't really *see* her. Fans of the Magnificent Marko might have remembered that he had an assistant – might even have remembered my name, if they'd been really pressed – but few of them would actually have been able to describe my face."

"And you wanted to perform," Luciana said, feeling a grudging kind of awe for the audacity of it all. "So you dressed as a man."

"It's not nearly as complicated as one might think. Now. I need a drink."

Morrell turned away, leaning heavily on her cane as she headed for the small table in the corner that held several glasses and a crystal decanter.

"The walking stick – it's not part of the act?" Luciana asked.

Morrell poured a drink and took a mouthful before turning back to Luciana again. She gave a grim smile. "If I didn't need it, I wouldn't be using dear Clara here as my assistant. I'd be doing the hard work myself, just like the old days."

Luciana shook her head. "I don't remember you having one when I saw you on stage."

Morrell sighed. "It was the Golden Butterfly," she said. "That trick was dangerous. I was still rehearsing, even on the morning of that fateful performance, and I messed it up. I missed my cue and fell straight into the orchestra pit.

Your grandfather wanted me to see a doctor, but I refused because I wanted to perform that night. I did and it was perfect." She swallowed the last of her drink and clunked the glass back down on to the table. "But the irony is that even if Thursby hadn't put the cat among the pigeons, that trick – and me – were both done for. I've not walked properly since. I would never have been able to do it again."

"I can't believe my grandfather would ever ask you to perform a trick that dangerous."

Morrell turned to her, another amused look on her face. "He didn't ask me," she said. "It was never his trick. It was *mine*. Half the tricks we performed were. That was the deal we had. Marko needed an assistant and I needed a magician who would let me perform – *really* perform. Not just do as he said, but actually come up with the illusions myself. Your grandfather never believed in the Grand Society's rules. He knew I was as good as he was. He saw that the first time I auditioned for him and he never once resented me for it. But he also knew I'd never be able to perform as myself, alone. We built his show together. I could never take the credit for what was rightfully mine, but at least I was working at my own illusions. At least I was doing what I loved, the way I wanted. I wasn't just some shill for a man who thought I was half what he was."

Luciana stared at her, too astonished to speak.

"When … when you say you came up with the illusions yourself," Charley ventured. "What do you mean, exactly?"

Morrell regarded him for a moment and then jerked her chin at Luciana's bag. "The rig you found. Give it back to me a moment."

Charley did as he was told. Morrell took the wing that still had most of the metal ribbon attached. She examined it for a moment.

"Let's see how good my workmanship is, shall we?" she asked with a wry smile.

With her free hand she gave the metal filament a hard tug. There was a click and a narrow metal arm sprung from either end of the outer edges of the triangle. Morrell held it up as more clicks sounded in the quiet room. The arm folded out, then folded out again, joint after joint snapping open and extending one after the other, *click-click-click-click-click*. In seconds, the golden wing had expanded far beyond its original size. Now the shape looked even more like a butterfly's wing. Inside the outer frame was a striation of thin, jointed golden metal struts that held the flimsy-looking apparatus rigid in Adeline Morrell's hand.

"It's clockwork," she said, once it was clear that the mechanism had finished opening. "My greatest achievement. My grandfather was a watchmaker, you see, and so was my father. He had no sons, so he taught me.

But when they had both passed on, even the men whose timepieces I had fixed while my father was alive decided that I was not capable on my own. *A woman's brain can't possibly understand the intricacies in a watch,* they said. And besides, *a woman can't run a business alone.* The work dwindled. So I built other things instead." She moved the solitary wing through the air. "I wore these under my costume. When they expanded beneath the fabric, they created the wings of the butterfly, as if they had grown out of my back, right there on stage. *I* am the heart of the trick. *I* am the Golden Butterfly."

Chapter Twenty-two

"There," said Morrell. "Now you know at least two of my secrets. What are you going to do with them?"

Luciana shook her head. "It wasn't true, was it? What my grandfather was accused of? That he had taught you magic?"

"No," Morrell agreed. "It wasn't. Though only because there was nothing he really needed to teach me. I always had a knack for it. I pick things up quickly, often just by watching, and more than that I can usually see a way to make it work better. Just the way my brain is, I suppose."

"He couldn't tell them the truth," Luciana realized. "Not without getting you into trouble. So he gave up his own career instead."

Adeline sighed. "He was a good man, your grandfather. One of the best. I miss him. I am sorry I was not at his funeral. Not that your grandmother would have welcomed me there."

"She didn't approve?" Luciana asked.

Morrell smiled faintly. "She is of a different generation," she said mildly. "One where women of her class sit and embroider in a safe corner so that they won't crease the silk of their skirts. Difference is not always easy to accept. I always respected her, but we never understood each other's viewpoint. So I simply tried to stay out of her way and she tried to stay out of mine. She never, at least, threatened to expose me, though Marko was always keen that she knew all his truths. That was the key to a happy marriage, he said." Morrell reached for the decanter again. "And anyway – I had much to be grateful to her for, despite our differences."

"Did Thursby know?" Charley asked. "That the trick was really yours, not Mr Cattaneo's?"

Adeline gave a short laugh. "Of course not. He would never have believed that a woman was capable of devising such a trick. Anyway, he just wanted the secret. He thought he could blackmail Marko into giving it to him, but it didn't work. I told Marko he should let it go. I broke the wings in two and gave him both pieces – I told him to give them to Thursby and let him work out the rest for himself, and good luck to him if he managed it. But Marko wouldn't. He maintained that the trick wasn't his to give, and that in any case, Thursby didn't deserve to have it. I had promised him I wouldn't go to Thursby with the truth, but I told myself that if he ever came to me and asked, I would tell him and it wouldn't be breaking my promise. But Thursby never bothered to come after me. I was only the assistant, after all. I assumed that Marko had destroyed them," she said, waving a dismissive finger at the open wing. "I never thought I'd see them again."

"Now that you have," Luciana said, "now that the wings have come back to you – why don't you use them again? No one's ever bettered that trick or even managed to replicate it. Thursby obviously never could. Recreate it and you'd be the greatest magician in the world. Everyone would want to see the Golden Butterfly! It would start a whole new age of magic!"

Adeline shook her head. "Never. That trick caused nothing but trouble. I wish I had never thought of it in the first place. There are too many reasons to leave it be. For one, this wing rig is broken, and making the mechanism again is just too difficult. Besides, the minute it appeared on my stage, Thursby would know I was more than I say I am. And I can't perform it myself – it would have to be

Clara. She's afraid of heights and I would never put her through that just for the sake of bruising Thursby's pride. No, the Golden Butterfly will never take to the air again, and good riddance. I should take the pieces of it and throw them in the Thames. Let the mudlarks find them and puzzle at what they are. I will never understand why Marko kept them in the first place. What good did it do?"

"Maybe he hoped that one day things would be different," suggested Luciana. "Maybe he thought that one day you might be able to perform the trick again, as yourself. But hiding things away won't change the way they are, will it? Perhaps he realized that after you'd broken them, and that's why he taught me what I needed to follow the trail."

Adeline Morrell frowned at that, as if contemplating the truth of Luciana's words. "What do you mean, he left a trail?"

"He put the first wing somewhere he knew only I could find it," Luciana told her. "The second clue we found in your room at the Peacock. That took us to Philpot Danvers. I don't know why *he* had one of Grandfather's puzzle boxes, especially since it was another one with a key that only I would know. That led us to the second part of the device."

"Philpot Danvers?" Morrell asked. She glanced at Clara, who had paled a little.

"We know he's one of Thursby's spies," Luciana said. "My grandfather knew that too. That's why I can't understand how he had one of his puzzle boxes. Danvers said it was a gift, but I don't believe him."

"You're right not to," said Morrell. "Marko would never have given Thursby's lapdog anything willingly. He must have stolen it."

"Maybe it was in the box that Thursby took from your grandfather's dressing room," Charley suggested. "Didn't Mr Hibberd say there was someone else with him when he searched it? It could have been Danvers, couldn't it?"

Luciana nodded. "I bet that's exactly where he got it from!"

"Didn't you say that you found the clue that lead you to him in my old room?" Adeline asked. "Where did you find it?"

"It was in the hidden space behind the cupboard in your dressing room," Luciana explained. "It was inside another puzzle box."

Morrell looked away, a faint smile on her face. "Well, well. Marko, that cunning old magician. I put that box there myself after it had all happened. He sent it to me, asking me to return it to the Peacock, where it belonged, and hide it somewhere no one would find it. I thought he was just being sentimental – that he wanted to leave a piece of our show in the fabric of the theatre forever more. So I put it in that secret little hiding place."

Luciana watched her carefully. "It was a box I remember playing with when I was very young," she said. "And I also think I remember being inside that hidden space, but I don't know why I would have been there."

"I probably showed it to you at some point," Morrell said, busying herself with the golden wings instead of meeting Luciana's eye. "Sometimes I would look after you when you were very small, if both of your grandparents were busy." She pushed back the metal ribbon she had used to activate the wing. The clockwork arms folded into themselves and then back into the metal casing. Then she handed both pieces to Luciana, who slipped them into her bag.

"I learned a lot from my grandfather," Luciana went on. "Some things he taught me deliberately. How to handle a deck of cards or how to pull a coin from someone's ear, for example. But other things he didn't have to teach me directly, because I pick things up quickly. Just by watching."

Adeline's face took on a guarded look. "Marko was so proud of you," she said quietly. "He loved you very much. You were so lucky that they took you in."

"I never knew my parents," said Luciana, still watching

the magician's face. "I've never even seen a photograph. Grandmother never liked to talk about them."

Morrell smiled. "Sometimes, after all, that's for the best."

"Is it?" Luciana asked. "Better for whom?"

"For everyone," Adeline said softly. "Because the answers we get aren't always the ones we want to hear."

There was a brief silence, which was broken by Clara.

"What are we going to do?" she asked, still leaning against the door. "We have a performance tonight. Are we going to go through with it, or—"

Adeline Morrell threw back her shoulders, raised her chin and took a deep breath. "But of course! The show must go on, isn't that right? Unless Miss Cattaneo here has some objection, I shall replace the nose of dear Adolphus and carry on as planned."

"I just wish we could stay and watch," Luciana said quietly.

"Well, I for one am glad you cannot," Morrell declared, stooping to sweep her discarded false nose from the floor. "It wouldn't do to lose any of my tricks to a sharp-eyed youth, would it?" She rested the hand holding the nose on her hip, her other curled around the silver head of her cane. "Will you go home?"

"If we haven't missed the last train," Charley said. "Yes, we will."

Morrell nodded. "Probably best not to mention me to your grandmother," she said quietly.

Luciana shook her head. "Neither of us will ever mention you to anyone. Not the real you, anyway."

The magician smiled rather sadly. "I believe you."

*

Outside, it had started to snow again, but Luciana didn't feel the cold as she and Charley made their way towards Charing Cross. She didn't feel anything.

"Are you all right?" Charley asked. "I thought you'd be happier."

"Why?" Luciana asked. "What do I have to be happy about?"

"You solved the mystery," Charley pointed out. "You worked out those puzzles when no one else could and now you know what the device is. You know what happened to your grandfather too, and why. Isn't that a good thing?"

Luciana stared at the lights that were blooming in the darkness falling over the city streets. "It hasn't answered anything," she said. "Not really. Am I supposed to feel clever now? What use is that?"

"What else were you hoping for?" Charley asked.

"Where did you think this would lead, Luciana?"

She shook her head. "It just feels as if all this should *change* something. *I* feel changed. But Thursby will just carry on, bullying people and squashing anyone who might perform great magic, and the Magnificent Marko will still be forgotten – and so will Adeline Morrell. And I have to go back to Grandmother and that big empty house and sit there in a corner in a silk skirt, trying not to ruffle it, just like Adeline said."

"What are you talking about?" Charley asked. "Your grandmother isn't like that."

"Yes she is!" Luciana said, stopping and turning to face Charley. "She wants me to have a safe life, and I don't *want* that. Not any more. "

"I don't see what's wrong with being safe," Charley argued. "Especially not if 'safe' means never having to worry about having a roof over your head or food on the table. A lot of people would love to have that. And you've always loved Midford and your grandparents' house, haven't you?"

"Of course I have," Luciana said. "I still do. But now … there's so much out here, Charley. So much I could *do*. I want what Adeline has – what Clara has. I want to be my own person, not stuck on a path someone else has laid out for me."

"Do you really think Adeline is being her own person?"

Charley asked. "She has to wear someone else's face – someone else's clothes – every single day."

"I don't think she's wearing someone else's clothes," said Luciana. "And if wearing someone else's face means she can do what she wants – can be who she wants to be – then maybe that's not such a bad thing."

Charley sighed. "Ana, look. You are capable of being whatever you want to be. I know you are. But right now – right at this moment – we *have* to go home. *Please.*"

"All right," she said, feeling cold and defeated. "Let's go."

They started to walk again, the cold slush washing up against their feet. Ahead of them a figure stepped out of an alleyway, the dark bulk of him blocking the light.

"Well, well, well," said Turner. "Just look what I've found."

Chapter Twenty-three

"What do you want?" Charley asked.

"Oh, I think you know." Turner nodded at Luciana's bag. "Hand it over."

Luciana backed away. "Leave us alone."

"I don't think so," Turner snarled. "You stole from Mr Danvers and now he wants recompense. Come on – give it up."

"He gave us that money!" Charley protested. "We didn't steal anything."

"He gave it to you so that you could go home," Turner pointed out. "From where Mr Danvers would have been able to come and retrieve the Golden Butterfly at his leisure on behalf of Mr Thursby. But no matter. Here you are and I can save them both the trouble."

Turner lunged at Luciana. She screamed and Charley tried to intervene. The three of them struggled in the darkness.

"Oi," said another voice. "What's happening here then?"

Luciana looked up to see a policeman coming towards them.

"Oh!" she said. "I'm so glad you're here – please—"

"These two ragamuffins have stolen my bag, officer!" boomed Turner, drowning out Luciana's voice.

"What?" Luciana gasped.

"That's a lie!" spluttered Charley. "He's the one who—"

The momentary interruption gave Turner exactly the second of distraction that he needed. He yanked the bag from Luciana's arms and walked swiftly away.

"Thank you, officer!" he threw over his shoulder. "I'm much obliged to you!"

"Wait!" cried Luciana. Both she and Charley tried to follow, but the policeman held them back.

"Now, now, now," he said. "That's enough of that."

"He was stealing from *us*," Luciana shouted, "and you've just helped him to do it!"

"Oh ho, so that's how it was, was it?" The copper scoffed. "The gent in the cap and smart suit was the one that nicked a bag off two children who look as if they haven't seen a bath in a month. A likely story."

The policeman refused to believe Luciana and Charley's true version of events. Even leaving out the bits involving magicians and puzzle boxes, it was hardly surprising. Finally Luciana realized that the only way they were going to get away was by running. She picked a moment when the copper was occupied with Charley and kicked out sharply with her booted foot, catching his shin. He gave a sharp yell and stumbled backwards.

"Run!" she yelled.

"You just injured a policeman!" Charley hissed, as they reached the end of the alleyway.

"He wasn't going to let us go," Luciana said, as they hurried into the dark tangle of streets that surrounded the station. She thought she should probably feel scared – after all, she'd just kicked a policeman! She did feel a bit guilty – she hoped the man's ankle wouldn't hurt for too long. But she felt far more guilty about what had transpired before the policeman had even arrived. She'd lost the Golden Butterfly, and in the worst possible way. It was on its way to Thursby even now – she'd let it go into the hands of the one person her grandfather had been desperate to keep it away from.

"Well, what are we going to do now?" Charley asked. "We don't have any money left to get a train to Rotherton!"

"We have to go back," Luciana said, home the last thing on her mind. "We have to warn Adeline and Clara."

*

By the time they had returned to the theatre, the evening's audience had begun to file in and the stage door was locked fast. Luciana hammered on it until Ben the stagehand pulled it open.

"What are you doing back?" he asked. "I can't let you in, it's nearly time for the performance!"

"You have to!" Luciana gasped, out of breath from running all the way. "We have to warn them that Thursby has the Golden Butterfly!"

Ben frowned in puzlement. "*Who* has the *what* now?"

"Just let us in, Ben," Charley said. "It's important."

The boy reluctantly stood to one side and Luciana and Charley ran down the corridor. Clara was coming towards them and shushed them as they called to her, ushering them into the magician's room. Once inside, Luciana explained what had happened. She wanted to speak to Adeline, but the magician had replaced her disguise and was once again Adolphus Merritt.

"He can't speak to you," Clara whispered. "The theatre is filling up ready for tonight's performance. There are people everywhere. If anyone was passing and happened to hear…"

"I understand," Luciana said, "but what do we do?"

Clara and Merritt shared a brief look. Then the

magician turned away and his assistant led Luciana and Charley out.

"Come," she said. She took them to her own small dressing room and waved them inside before shutting the door firmly behind them. "Listen to me. The Golden Butterfly doesn't matter. If Thursby's got it – well, good luck to him. I warrant it won't do him any good – even if he puzzles it out, the device is only half the trick. Anyway, you heard what Adeline said – it's broken, even if he knew what to do with it. All that matters now is *this* performance. *Our* performance. Do you understand? This is our life, our livelihood. Exposure would mean disaster – for both of us. People aren't interested in magic any more, and we've worked so very hard to get this billing. We're building an audience, a reputation. We can't lose it now for the sake of a trick that she cares nothing for."

Luciana looked down at her toes, feeling utterly hopeless. "But I was supposed to keep it safe, and instead all I've done is pass it straight into Thursby's hands. And to think that he's finally got what he wanted, without even having to work for it and after what he did to my grandfather. After what he did to *her*. Driving them from the stage, taking what they loved, what they had both worked for—"

Clara rested a hand on her shoulder. "It's not your fault, Luciana. You can't think like that. Only Thursby is in the wrong here. And I understand your anger. Really, I do. But you don't want it all to happen again, do you?"

Luciana shook her head miserably. "It's so unfair," she said. "This isn't how it should be."

Clara straightened up again with a sad smile. "No, it isn't. But this is how it is, and we will learn to make the best of it. Now, I've got to get ready. The two of you can watch the show from backstage, if you like. We'll find you somewhere to bed down afterwards, and tomorrow we will make sure you get home."

Luciana wanted to protest. She no more wanted to return home now than she had before she'd lost the Golden Butterfly. But Clara was already bustling to her wardrobe, pulling out her stage costume.

"At least you get to do one trick yourself," Luciana murmured. "Even if no one believes that it's you doing it."

"Oh," Clara said with a brief laugh. "I won't be doing that again. If you saw it, then others will too, eventually. We can't risk one of those being Thursby. It was foolish of me in the first place, to risk so much just because of my pride."

Luciana's heart sank. "It's so unfair. More than that, it's – it's absurd!"

Clara turned with a smile. "Well, perhaps one day, things will be different. Now, I have to change."

Later, as they stood in the shadowed darkness of the wings and watched Adolphus Merritt weave another performance, Charley pressed his lips to her ear.

"There are just as many women out there in the audience as men," he whispered. "Maybe even more. Surely all of them would watch a woman magician, even if their husbands would protest."

"Perhaps," Luciana whispered back. "But it would be their husbands who had the money to buy the tickets."

Charley drew back and looked at her, as if this hadn't occurred to him. "That can't be completely true," he said, still whispering. "My mother is the one who earns for us."

Luciana nodded with a frown. "That's true. But would she spend money coming to the theatre?"

Charley shrugged. "I don't know. Perhaps she would if she knew she was going to see a woman on stage."

Luciana sighed. "Maybe. Maybe not."

Charley looked out at Adolphus Merritt and Clara. "It's a pity, isn't it?" he asked. "It's a pity that she doesn't get to choose for herself."

Luciana watched too. *None of us do*, she thought. *None of us ever will, all the time that people like Thursby are in charge. And when will that ever change?*

Luciana watched the rest of Adeline's performance in silence, feeling more hopeless by the minute. She'd solved all her grandfather's puzzles and she'd used her own magic skills to get here. But what good had it done? All she'd succeeded in doing was discovering a life she couldn't have and had handed over her grandfather's greatest trick to a horrible imposter in the process.

Chapter Twenty-four

That night her dream of fire was worse than ever. Luciana tossed and turned, finally roused from a fitful sleep by a hurried knocking on Clara's dressing-room door. She opened it to find Ben the stagehand standing outside, breathing hard.

"Miss Luciana!"

"Ben!" Luciana said. "What on earth's the matter?"

There was a noise further down the corridor and Charley stuck his head out of a room, his hair mussed. "What's going on?" he asked. "It's not even six o'clock yet!"

"It's this," Ben said, pulling a folded sheet of paper from his pocket. "I went out to get a bite for breakfast but when I saw it I knew it couldn't wait. This is what you were talking about yesterday, wasn't it? The Golden Butterfly and Thursby."

He passed it to Charley, who unfolded it as he reached Luciana's side. It was a quarter-sized playbill of the sort that hawkers passed out on the street to tout for trade. Luciana and Charley stared dumbly at the creased yellow sheet.

Behold!

Come See the Extraordinary Skill of Carl Thursby!
The Greatest Magician Alive Returns to the Stage!

It was the next lines, though, that truly made Luciana gasp.

Be Amazed!
Be Astonished!
Be Flabbergasted by:
The Golden Butterfly!
The Greatest Illusion of Our Age!

"But how?" Luciana asked, horrified. "How did he unravel the trick so fast? How can he be ready to perform it just hours after he got hold of the wings?"

"Maybe he's not," Ben suggested. He pointed at the performance date. "Look. That date's for the Tuesday after next. That's more'n a week away, ain't it? He's eager to thump up a buzz, but he's given himself plenty of breathing space."

Luciana grabbed the paper and stared, her mind

working overtime as she clutched at whatever remaining hope she could. "You're right. So maybe there's still a way to stop him! Perhaps we can find the wings and – I don't know – steal them back again! After all, we know where they're going to be! He'll be rehearsing at the theatre every hour of every day between now and then, won't he?"

Charley looked alarmed. "Ana, we can't do that!"

"Why not?" she asked defiantly, the tide of despair that had crept over her the previous evening beginning to recede, excitement taking its place. "He stole them! Why shouldn't I take them back?"

"Because this isn't who we are," Charley said tiredly. "Ana, all this … all this running about, plotting and scheming and adventuring. It's not who we are."

"It might not be who *you* are," Luciana retorted, determined not to let this chance slip through her fingers. "But it's who I am. I'll do it on my own if I have to. You can go back to your nice *safe* life and be a gardener if you like, but that's not enough for me."

Luciana wished she could call her words back again as soon as she had said them, but it was too late.

"All right," Charley said. "You're right. I'm the one who doesn't belong here. I should go back. I've probably still got just enough coppers to get myself a ticket."

Charley turned and left the room just as quietly as he'd

spoken. Luciana listened to his footsteps padding softly down the hallway. The silence in her room reigned for a few more minutes as she tried to quell the sick feeling that was bubbling in her stomach.

"You ever stolen anything before?" Ben asked into the quiet a moment later. "Cos it ain't as easy as people think. And I wouldn't recommend it if there's any other way."

"What other way could there possibly be?"

Ben shrugged. "You know what theatrical types really hate? Being upstaged. What you need to do is to rain on his parade."

Luciana stared at the paper. She wasn't listening to Ben. She was listening to the sound of Charley's footsteps as he left.

*

"He won't be ready to perform it in a week," said Clara, as she and Adeline – perfectly made up as Merritt once more – looked at the playbill. "He can't be. It wouldn't be safe. The mechanism is broken."

"Perhaps he knows a way to fix it?" Luciana suggested. "That must be possible, somehow?"

Merritt raised his arms in a shrug that said *maybe*.

"Well, we have to do something," Luciana said, determined. "We can steal the devices back."

"Oh no," said Clara. "That's a terrible idea."

"All right then," Luciana said. "*You* stage the trick yourself before he has a chance to perform it. The Saturday before him, say. Upstage him so well that there would be no point in him doing it himself."

The magician actually laughed at that, although it was entirely silent. He took out a notepad and pen and scribbled for a moment. *I told you,* he wrote, *there was only ever one set of the wings. They took me months to make. What do you expect me to do? Build a new set in less than a week?*

"You don't have the wings any more," Clara ventured. "But what about my angel?"

Merritt looked up at Clara with a frown, then wrote another note. *That's not the same thing at all.*

"Isn't it?" Clara asked. "As I understand it, it works the same way, or very nearly."

"The angel?" Luciana asked. "What's that?"

It's nothing, wrote the magician, moving away from them both.

"It's a mechanical wonder," Clara said. "Merritt made it as a Christmas present for me. A little toy angel about as high as my knee with wings that fold out from its back. I thought of it the minute I saw that broken wing opening. It's exactly the same principle, isn't it? The wings are built in the same way. They're just smaller and a different shape."

Merritt bit his lip for a moment, then scribbled some more. *Yes, it is. But that doesn't mean I could take them from the angel and use them for this trick. Anyway, the proportions would be wrong. They'd look tiny on you, Clara. And even if it could work, I'd never let you do this trick, not with your fear of heights.*

"Then I'll do it," said Luciana.

Chapter Twenty-five

Clara and Merritt both turned to look at her, astonished.

"What?" Clara exclaimed. "Don't be ridiculous!"

"Why is it ridiculous?" Luciana pressed. "I'm not afraid of heights. I'm not afraid to try. Just imagine the interest it would generate if the granddaughter of the greatest magician in the world were to step on to the stage and recreate his greatest trick, the trick that finished his career. The theatre would be full. Wouldn't it? No one would give Thursby's show another thought."

And then what? Merritt asked. *Thursby would be even more incensed.*

"So what?" Luciana asked.

The magician shook his head, and continued to write

as Luciana watched.

I can't have him scrutinizing me in any way. You must realize that! In fact, I'd rather he didn't notice me at all. I've been very deliberate in our act – nothing too flashy, nothing too clever or different or new. All because I don't want Thursby to bother with me. Understand?

"Because he might realize you're a woman?" Luciana asked.

"Keep your voice down," Clara hissed.

Adeline stared at her from the face of Adolphus Merritt. Then the magician leaned forward and whispered in Luciana's ear so quietly she had to strain to hear the words.

"That's only part of it," Merritt said seriously. "You don't know Thursby, Luciana. You don't know what he's capable of. What you're asking me to do – I can't. It's too dangerous. I'd be calling Thursby out for the biggest fool in the world, and it wouldn't just be me in his sights. He'd go out of his way to destroy me and everyone around me."

"Then fight *back*," Luciana said, stepping back. "I don't understand why nobody stands up to Thursby. And isn't this a perfect opportunity? I understand that you're worried about risking your livelihood, I really do. But sooner or later, someone's going to work out who you really are. If I did, others can too. Why not make it count, instead of just waiting for it to happen? Make it matter. Make it yours.

Perform the Golden Butterfly, and then reveal yourself to be Adeline Morrell. How could anyone say a woman can't perform magic then? You'd have already proved them wrong. Thursby would be finished."

Merritt shook his head and picked up his pen.

You are asking too much, Luciana.

Luciana's heart sank, but the magician hadn't finished writing.

I can't shed this face, the magician went on. *Adolphus Merritt is here to stay. But ... if you really aren't afraid to try the trick yourself... Perhaps we could consider that.*

Luciana's heart leaped. "I'm not. Truly, I'm not."

Merritt turned away, deep in thought. After a moment he turned back and wrote another note.

We don't have much time. If we're to have any hope of succeeding, we're going to have to start right now.

Clara sighed. "We'll have to be very careful," she said. "We'd have to get Ben to keep a note of everyone coming and going. Maybe even ask Mr Phipps to get extra security. Meanwhile," she said to Luciana, "the first thing *you* have to do is actually stand on the stage."

*

Clara led Luciana out into the great cavern that was the stage. The curtains had been lifted and she could see directly out into the auditorium. Seats stretched back into the darkness. The balconies gleamed a dull gold from the lights overhead. Empty, the theatre seemed so much bigger than it had when Luciana herself had sat in the audience.

"Try to imagine it full," Clara said quietly, into the expansive silence of the place.

Luciana swallowed. "There are so many seats…"

Clara squeezed her shoulder.

Luciana took a deep breath and tried to centre her thoughts, but something was bothering her.

"What did A—" she had to stop herself, almost saying the wrong name. "*Adolphus* mean, when he said that I didn't know what Thursby is capable of? Why is he so afraid of him?"

Clara frowned. "I don't want to scare you. And really, they're just rumours. No one has ever been able to prove anything."

"I'd rather know. I'm the one who's going to be out here, aren't I?"

The assistant sighed. "All right. Magicians that Thursby doesn't get on with have a habit of having … unfortunate accidents."

Luciana remembered the fear that had coiled in her stomach when she'd first met Thursby.

"What do you mean?" she asked, her voice thick.

Clara rubbed a hand over her face. "I don't really want to tell you details, Luciana. But several theatres have burned down. One fellow's horse spooked and threw him, breaking his back in three places. Unpleasant, terrible incidents."

Clara's mention of fire brought Luciana's nightmare of the night before back again in a flash that made her catch her breath. It had been her in the flames this time, surrounded by burning walls that blocked her every escape. She swallowed hard.

"Her leg," she said. "Was that…"

"No, that was a genuine accident. But the murmurs were that it perhaps saved your grandfather a worse fate than the one he ended up with."

"What do you mean?"

"Two accidents in close succession at the same theatre might have been a little too suspicious. Especially given poor Adeline's history." Clara saw Luciana's questioning look and sighed again. "Adeline was married once. Her husband was a magician – the first double act of which she was part. They were very good, by all accounts. Too good, perhaps. He died when the theatre they had been performing in caught fire, poor soul. Adeline herself only just escaped the flames."

For a moment, the darkness at the edge of the stage seemed to reach up and tangle Luciana in its depths. She felt as if she were falling into a dark pit, and at the base of it was her greatest nightmare. She saw a man engulfed in fire, burnt, burning—

"Luciana?" Clara asked, gripping her arm, looking worried. "Are you all right? You look as if you're about to faint."

"Well, well, well," boomed a voice from the darkened wings. "What's happening here? A private tour? You know I don't allow that. If someone wants to come into my theatre, they work or they pay the ticket price. No exceptions!"

They both turned to see a man with greying hair and a neat moustache stalking towards them. His face was pale, round, and bore a look of controlled annoyance. Luciana focused on him, willing her dream to dissipate.

"It's not a tour, Mr Phipps," Clara told him. "This is Luciana Cattaneo. She's Mr Merritt's newest assistant."

"Aha." Phipps picked up the monocle that hung on a chain around his neck and jammed it into one eye, squinting. He looked Luciana up and down and then glanced at Clara. "Replacing you already, is he? What have you done, girl?"

Clara coloured a little. "Oh no, Mr Phipps. I'm not leaving the show. Luciana is an additional assistant."

Mr Phipps's eyebrows rose in surprise. His monocle dropped back on to its chain. "An *additional* assistant! Well, he needn't think his fee will be increased to accommodate the extra help!"

"This is simply for a special performance, Mr Phipps. Luciana is the granddaughter of the Magnificent Marko. She is going to step on to the stage as part of a great illusion that will honour his memory. He died recently, you know."

Phipps picked up his monocle again, peering through it at Luciana with renewed interest. "Is she, by Jove? Well, well, well. That will bring the punters in. And when is this illustrious performance going to take place?"

"On Saturday, Mr Phipps."

"Saturday!" Phipps straightened up. "Well then, where the devil is Merritt? He should be here rehearsing!"

As if on cue, the tapping of a cane sounded against the polished boards of the stage. Adolphus Merritt appeared out of the darkness. The magician walked towards them, chin up, calm gaze levelled directly at Mr Phipps.

"Ah," said Phipps, his bluster of moments before deflating. "There you are, my good man. Your girl here has told me all the details. Very good. We'll fill this place, what? I suppose that the girl's papers are all in order. Seal of approval from the Grand Society and whatnot. Of course they are, of course. Well, I shall leave you to get on with your work. Good day, ladies, gentleman."

With that he shuffled off into the darkness. Once his footsteps had echoed away, Clara turned to Merritt with an anxious look on her face.

"The licence! We hadn't thought of that! What are we going to do?"

Merritt took out his notepad. *Don't worry*, he wrote. *It's in hand.*

After their tour of the stage, Merritt went back to his dressing room while Clara returned to their digs to retrieve the angel. Luciana found herself alone again in Clara's room, which they had to share for the time Luciana was working at the theatre. She sat on the old chaise longue and looked around her, wondering what her grandfather would make of where she'd ended up. She wondered what Charley was doing at that moment too, and a fresh well of guilt and loneliness sprang into her gut. They'd never argued before, or at least not in earnest. Luciana knew it was her fault. It was hours since he'd left, so he was more than likely already home, which meant that it was also very likely that her grandmother now knew exactly where Luciana was. Would he, though, tell Isabella Cattaneo *who* she was with, truly? Charley had vowed to keep Adeline's secret, and Luciana had never once known her friend not to keep his word, but how far would that vow extend if the price of breaking it meant setting her grandmother's mind at rest? After all, the knowledge that her granddaughter was with an old friend of her grandfather's, even one of whom she disapproved, would surely be better than thinking that Luciana was with a complete stranger.

When Clara returned, her eyes were full of worry. Her clothes were wet with melting snow even though it shouldn't have been more than a ten-minute walk back from where she and the magician were staying.

"Someone was following me," she told Luciana and Merritt. "I think they were waiting outside our rooms when I came out. I took a detour to make sure they didn't tail me straight here."

"Did you see who it was?" Luciana asked, immediately suspecting Turner or Danvers.

Clara shook her head. "They were quick enough to stay out of my eyesight," she said.

"It must be one of Thursby's men," Luciana said.

"But if that's the case, why bother?" Clara asked. "Surely they already know the theatre where I am performing? Anyway, I didn't want to confront them, not when I was carrying this."

Clara put down the bag she carried over one shoulder and pulled out a large package wound in a white sheet, unwrapping it to reveal a porcelain doll dressed in a shimmering gold gown with a white cloak. In one slim hand she held a golden trumpet. Clara set her down on the edge of the table and then reached under the doll's blond locks. She gave a swift tug at something and there was an audible click.

As the three of them watched, a pair of wings appeared from the angel's back. They were a different shape to those of the Golden Butterfly, but they were recognizably the same type of construction. They unfolded gradually, with the same series of clicks, into wings that were larger than the angel herself – their shoulders higher than her head, their tails lower than her bare porcelain toes. The biggest difference though, was that as they opened, dozens of white feathers made of thin silk unfurled from around the wings' metal struts. By the time they were fully open, the little porcelain figure stood before them with a pair of white delicately feathered angel's wings.

"That's so clever!" Luciana exclaimed. "And the way you've done the feathers too! I've never seen anything like it, have—" She turned around, looking for Charley, because just for a moment she forgot he was no longer by her side, where he had always been. A lance of pain stabbed Luciana through the heart and she swallowed, hard, her eyes blurring with tears. She blinked, turning back to the angel, feeling wretched.

Adeline silently turned the doll around and parted her hair to show Luciana how the housing for the wings had been set directly into the angel's back. To remove them would require shattering her torso. The magician pointed to the tiny loop between them, at the top of the device. She drew an invisible line from the loop up to the ceiling.

"If we use these wings for the Golden Butterfly, that would be how they activate," Clara said quietly.

"I see," said Luciana, trying her best to recover. "A line comes down from above?"

Merritt nodded.

"It's … it's a very small loop," Luciana said, her voice quavering a little. For the first time, it occurred to her to be nervous. How she wished that Charley were there!

Clara reached out and took her hand, squeezing it gently. "You don't have to do this," she said.

Luciana looked directly into the face of Adolphus Merritt and took a deep breath. "Adeline Morrell did this. I can too."

The magician smiled.

Chapter Twenty-six

Clara, on Merritt's behalf, placed the entire building under lockdown – no one was allowed in or out and even Ben was under strict instructions not to come near the auditorium. Still the magician did not speak, relying instead on written notes and diagrams.

Luciana's first task had nothing to do with magic. She had to dance.

"To the audience it must seem as if you are enchanted," Clara advised her. "Raise your arms, spin, weave in and out of the light – be an apparition, a fairy."

Luciana did as she was told and started from the wings, taking a low turn on her tiptoes to move on to the stage. At first she wanted to ask what dancing had to do with magic. Then she realized that Merritt was standing at the other end of the stage with one hand raised. The magician's fingers flicked this way and that, mirroring the direction of her movements, as if the two were connected, and Luciana remembered how the Golden Butterfly had started that one and only time it had been performed: with Adeline coming on from the shadows in a trance.

Of course, Luciana thought. *The audience is to think that I am being controlled by Merritt's magic rather than moving of my own accord.*

After that, she found it easier to throw herself into the spectacle. She pretended that she could feel the pull of an invisible force wrapped around one wrist like a rope, coaxing her on to the stage.

"Very good!" Clara cried. "Stop now, for a moment. Come and try this."

Clara had been sitting to one side of the stage with a sewing kit and one of her stage costumes. It was made from length after length of diaphanous gold fabric that shimmered when the light hit it. Clara got to her feet and held the garment up to Luciana's shoulders.

"I think it will fit," Clara said. "It will still be long – you'll have to be careful not to tangle yourself in it as you dance."

"What about the angel's wings?" Luciana asked.

"How are we going to make that work?"

Merritt placed a hand on her shoulder and shook his head.

"All in good time," Clara told her with a warm smile. "Now, I've got to get up on to the bridge."

"The bridge?" Luciana asked, mystified.

Clara pointed into the darkness above them. Just visible was a criss-cross construction of wooden rafters that hung below the roof. It looked as if it were made of matchsticks and driftwood and it was very high. "That's where the line will drop from."

"But Merritt said you were scared of heights," Luciana whispered. The bridge was *very* high, and though she had no fear of heights herself, she knew what it was to be so terrified of something that you could hardly breathe for thinking about it.

Clara pressed her lips into a tight line, which was not close enough to a smile to be a denial. "I'll be all right. The show must go on, isn't that so? Don't worry about me. Just concentrate on what you have to do."

Luciana was humbled by Clara's bravery and determination. She watched the woman vanish into the darkness before turning to Merritt, guilt and worry churning in her heart.

"There must be another way," she said.

The magician took his notepad from his pocket and scribbled a quick sentence.

I trust Clara more than anyone else I know. I trust her with my life. More importantly I trust her with yours. Is there anyone you trust that much?

"Charley," she whispered painfully. "I trust Charley."

The magician nodded and gave a sad smile and a shrug. The meaning was clear. Charley wasn't here and so the only other option was dear, sweet, brave, terrified Clara.

*

They worked all afternoon and long into the evening, until Luciana was tired, hungry and irritable. It had taken poor Clara an age to make her way up to the rafters over the stage. Once she had secured the line she dropped it down to the stage. In unravelled silently and so invisibly that without the piece of scarlet ribbon secured to the end of it, neither Merritt not Luciana would have seen it at all. Merritt grasped the end of the line and measured the length it would need to be, then cut it off and attached a tiny silver hook before letting it go. It swung away from them. Luciana tried to follow its progress but it was almost impossible to see.

"How will I know where it is?" she asked. "I can't dance out on to the stage and then spend an age looking for it!"

Merritt smiled a little and made a circular, repeating motion with one finger. *Practice.*

And so they did, over and over until Luciana was dizzy with spinning, her feet hurt and she had a headache from searching the gloom of the stage for the line. She had no idea what time it was when the magician finally called a halt by clapping loudly and holding up his hands. He looked up into the rafters above and waved at Clara, hidden somewhere far above them.

Luciana collapsed in a heap in the middle of the stage, almost too tired to speak.

Clara reappeared a few minutes later, her face pale but with a smile plastered determinedly across it. When she pulled Luciana into a hug, the younger woman could feel her trembling.

"I'm so sorry," Luciana said, hugging her back, hard. "It's terrible that you have to do something that scares you so."

"It's all right," Clara told her. "The world is full of obstacles to be surmounted. Next time I will take one of my long scarves and tie myself to one of the rafters. That way at least I will know I *can't* fall, even if it feels as if I might." She looked up at Merritt. "You owe us both dinner, maestro, and a decent one at that."

Outside, the weather had swapped snow for the sort of

rain that pretends not to be there, so as to better insinuate itself between your collar and your neck. Luciana shivered as it settled on her cheeks. A shadow flickered into her periphery as they walked the gaslit street. It was gone by the time Luciana had turned towards it, but left the impression of a person, melting back into darkness.

They ate ham and eggs by dim candlelight in the fuggy bar of the Rising Sun on Winchurch Street. Merritt had a piece of paper and was sketching something. It looked like a draft of a playbill, but Luciana was too weary to ask. She was looking forward to curling up on the chaise longue in Clara's dressing room.

"Tomorrow we will rehearse with the dress," Clara told her. "We must see how well you can move in it, or whether I need to make more adjustments before we introduce the wings. I'll also take you up to the bridge so that you can get used to being up there. It takes some practice to stay still enough that no one notices you."

Luciana yawned widely and Clara grinned around a mouthful of her food.

"I don't know how you do it every day," Luciana admitted. "I'm so tired I can barely eat."

"Well, it's not every day," Clara said, pointing at the large clock on the wall with her knife. "You'll notice we're not on stage tonight, for example. We never perform on Mondays.

But yes, it's hard work. Especially for the assistants. It's far gentler a life on the magicians themselves."

Merritt looked up at that, arching an eyebrow above eyes that twinkled with laughter as Clara jabbed him in the ribs with an elbow, laughing too. Luciana felt a jolt. The expression in the magician's eyes seemed familiar and she knew that it belonged entirely to Adeline, rather than to Adolphus. When dressed so meticulously as the magician it was easy for Luciana to forget who was beneath it all, but every now and then a flash of memory took her by surprise. No, she couldn't even think of it as a memory – it was just a feeling, a sensation that there was something Luciana had once known but had now forgotten. In a flash, she heard Adeline's voice:

Sometimes, after all, it is better not to know.

Her face must have given her away at that moment, for Clara reached over and placed her hand over Luciana's. "Are you all right?"

Luciana looked at Merritt. Those blue eyes studied her carefully. Luciana wanted to say something, to ask a question, but the pub was crowded and who knew who was listening? And what, exactly, did she want to ask?

"Just tired," she said eventually.

Chapter Twenty-seven

Outside, the rain had taken on an edge of ice. They hurried along with their heads bowed until, at the corner of Nuttall Street, the magician motioned for them both to stop. He made two small gestures with his hands that indicated they should go ahead of him.

Clara complied with no more than a nod, tucking Luciana's hand into the crook of her elbow and then striking up a bright line of chat as they continued to walk. Luciana looked back but could see nothing save the dark pools between the gaslights and the indistinct shapes of the buildings looming into the night.

"Don't worry," Clara murmured, "Merritt knows what he's doing."

She led them around another corner and a moment or two later there was a muffled shout behind them, followed by a brief scuffle. Clara and Luciana turned to see the magician tussling with a smaller figure, both of them obscured by shadow.

"Stop it!" shouted the smaller figure. "Get off me!"

Luciana gasped. She knew that voice!

"Charley?"

The magician grasped the boy by the shoulders, turning his face to the meagre light which was filtering down with the cold rain. Charley was shivering, his hair and face wet, his sodden clothes hanging heavy on his small frame.

"Oh!" Luciana ran to him and threw her arms about his neck, hugging hard. "What are you doing here? Why aren't you back home in Midford?"

"I went t-to the st-station, but I c-couldn't b-bring myself to b-buy a ticket," Charley said, stuttering with cold. "C-couldn't just l-leave you h-here with strangers."

"So it's you who's been following us?" Clara asked. "But why?"

Charley pulled away from Luciana and looked her in the face. "I k-know y-you don't w-want me h-here," he said. "B-but I l-love you, L-Luciana. Y-you're f-family t-t-to me. I h-had to be s-sure you w-were s-safe, e-even if I h-had t-to do it in s-s-secret."

Luciana's eyes filled with tears and she hugged him again. "You're family to me too. I'm so sorry for what I said. I didn't mean it, Charley. I really didn't. Come on. We've got to get you into dry clothes before you catch your death."

Back at the theatre, they persuaded Ben to give up his second pair of trousers with the promise that they'd get him a brand-new pair at the earliest opportunity. Merritt pulled out a shirt and a jacket of his own – too big, of course, but better than the wet mess that Charley's had become.

"I can't believe you've been out there at all hours in that weather," Luciana said, once he was in dry clothes and the two of them were sat in front of a fire in the magician's dressing room. Every time Luciana looked at the flames, the fire threatened to bring back her dream again, but she refused to give in to the fear. It was more important for her to sit beside Charley as it warmed him. Besides, with him there, she felt as if she could defeat anything. "Where were you planning to sleep?"

"I saw that boy who took us to the Peacock at Charing Cross and asked him if he had a place I could stay. He said he'd wait until ten past closing time and if I needed somewhere he'd take me to where he sleeps. I think it's under the station somewhere."

Luciana shook her head. "You should have gone home. I wouldn't have blamed you. I'm so sorry that I said you didn't belong. I didn't mean it. The thing is, I'm not even sure I was talking about you. I think I was talking about myself, really."

Charley gave her a confused look. "What do you mean?"

Luciana was quiet for a moment, trying to assemble the right words in the head. She felt she needed to explain, but to do that she had to go right back to the beginning.

"Just after we found the first part of the Golden Butterfly, something happened with my grandmother," she began. "She … wanted to talk to me about you. She said we were on different paths and that we'd get further and further apart as we got older. It was so confusing. Scary too. It felt as if with Grandfather gone, everything was changing and I didn't have any say over any of it. I think that's one reason why I was so determined to solve the puzzles and save the Golden Butterfly. It's all part of my past, when everything felt … I don't know, *right*. Then we found Adeline and Clara, and in a funny kind of way everything made sense again. And now, if I can do this – if I can make the Golden Butterfly work – then maybe everything will be all right, whatever the future brings. Does that make any sense?"

Charley frowned. "I think so."

"You're the best friend I've got, Charley," Luciana told him. "It's always been us, together. But this … this is something I must do. I *have* to. I can't just go back home to Midford and forget about it. Not yet."

Charley sighed and looked around the dressing room. "I used the last of the money to send a telegram back home, to let them know that we're safe. I didn't tell them where we are, just that we were with old friends of your grandfather's and that they shouldn't worry."

"Thank you."

Charley looked back to her, a serious look on his face. "They will worry anyway though. You realize that, don't you?"

Luciana dipped her head, ashamed. "I know. But—"

"—this is just something you have to do," Charley finished for her.

"I can't let Thursby win," she said, desperate for him to understand. "Not just for me, but for Adeline and my grandfather too. He took Marko's profession away from him. He took Adeline's whole life. Now he's taken her invention and he wants to take the limelight, just when she's made a new life and a new name for herself. It's not right. There's nothing I can do to change the past, Charley, or the fact that my grandfather's gone, but I *know* I can do this."

Charley reached out and squeezed her hand. He still felt cold, although he'd stopped shivering. "I know. I do understand Luciana. And if it's what you have to do … then I'll help. I'd rather do that than trust someone else to look out for you."

There was a brief knock at the door before it opened. Luciana was surprised to see Adeline Morrell walk through the door, all trace of Adolphus Merritt scrubbed away. She smiled at Luciana's expression.

"It's past midnight. Even Ben is fast asleep. The only people here are the ones who know me for who I really am. Charley, are you feeling better?"

"Yes, thank you."

Adeline drew up a chair and sat down beside the fire. "Look, Luciana, I have been impressed by you today. You have worked so hard. But tomorrow will be harder, and the day after that harder still. We haven't even started working with the wire yet, and that's where the danger really comes in. We can stop now. We don't need to do this. You can both go home."

Luciana and Charley looked at each other. "No," Luciana said. "I'm not going home. I'm not going anywhere. I want to do this."

Morrell took a deep breath, and then held something out: a scroll of white paper.

"All right then," she said. "In that case, you should look at this. If you're really sure you want to do this, I'll take this to the printer in the morning."

Luciana took the paper and unfurled it. It was a design for a playbill, announcing:

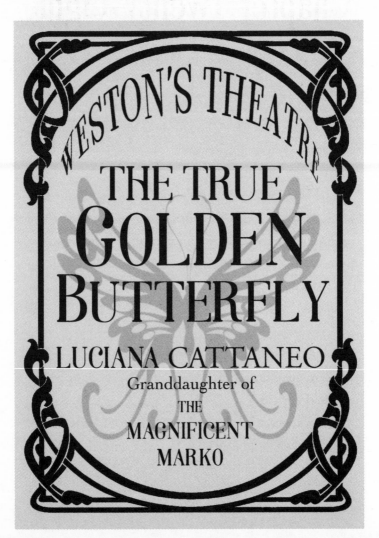

WESTON'S THEATRE

THE TRUE
GOLDEN
BUTTERFLY

LUCIANA CATTANEO

Granddaughter of

THE

MAGNIFICENT

MARKO

Chapter Twenty-eight

The next day Clara fitted Luciana into the dress she would wear for the performance. The fabric was nowhere near as light as Luciana had imagined it would be. It tangled around her legs as she spun, it conspired to trip her as she leaped. It made reaching the goal of the wire and hook even harder.

While she struggled below, Merritt and Charley laboured above. They climbed up to the rafters with a toolbox and a winch, and for several hours all that could be heard overhead was banging and clattering as the pair of them fixed it into place. The line vanished and Merritt reappeared on the stage, though without Charley. The magician indicated that Luciana should climb up into the rafters herself.

"He's right," Clara added. "You need to get used to being up there too. No – don't change. Keep the costume on."

"But how am I to climb in it?" Luciana asked.

"Barefoot and as best you can," Clara answered. "And do try not to tear it!"

The ladders that led up above the stage were bolted flat against the rear walls. By the time she reached the point where she had to cross from the first to a second, Luciana's arms ached, her feet hurt, and she was hot and tired. As she reached the bridge and began crawling on hands and knees to Charley, she decided she was sick of the whole venture.

"So," he said cheerfully, as he sat on one beam, dangling his legs. There was a single lit candle on the rafter beside him, casting his face in a weird glow. Luciana tried not to think about how close it was to the wooden beam. She wouldn't ask Charley to work in the dark, not this high off the stage, however afraid she was of what a stray flame could do to that wooden structure, no matter that she'd had her nightmare every night since she'd been in London. "How are you enjoying being a magician's assistant so far?"

"It's just plain horrible," she grumbled as she reached his side.

"Watching you from all the way up here, dancing in

that glittering cloth, you look like a ghost, or a sprite," Charley said. "It's quite eerie."

"Well, I don't feel like a sprite," she said. "Right now I feel more like an old dish rag."

Charley laughed and bumped her shoulder. "You're not scared to be up here then?"

"A little dizzy when I look down, perhaps, but not scared."

"That's good."

Luciana nodded to the winch. The line had been fed around it. "Show me how that works."

Charley cranked the handle clockwise and the mechanism turned smoothly as the line dropped towards the stage. He wound it anticlockwise and it came back up again. It was completely silent.

"I'll have to keep it well oiled," he said. "Can't have any sudden squeaks or jerks that'd give the game away."

Luciana watched as Charley repeated the movement and the line with the hook on dropped quickly towards the stage below. She tried to imagine being on the end of that line, being pulled upwards into these rafters. It seemed like a very long way up – and down.

"When you get here, I have to grab you and pull you on to this beam," Charley told her. "Then we both have to sit here, still as statues with no bits of us showing, until

209

the curtain comes down at the end of the show. Oh, and just to make it a fraction more of a challenge," he added, leaning over and blowing out the candle so that the space around them sputtered into darkness, "we have to do it in the pitch-black. Merritt says we'll have a blanket to cover us completely on the night."

"Wonderful," said Luciana.

Charley grinned. "All right then. We'd better start rehearsing the next bit. I've got to be able to pull you all the way up from the stage as smoothly as a bubble rising through beer."

"It'll be harder with me on the end of it," Luciana observed.

"Best get cracking then." he said. "Although this won't be the first time I've held you on a rope now, will it?"

*

When they broke for a quick lunch Merritt went out, returning sometime later with two parcels – a small one wrapped in what looked like an old woollen scarf and another large oblong one wrapped in sturdy brown paper. The magician unwrapped the larger one first. Inside were the printed playbills, resplendent with red and black printing against a stark white background.

Luciana and Charley looked at it together. Neither of

them said anything for a while. Luciana's name stood out in very large scarlet letters.

"What do you think?" Clara asked. "It looks good, doesn't it?"

"Very good," Charley agreed, although Luciana could tell he was thinking the same as her: that suddenly this all seemed a lot more real.

Merritt unwrapped the other parcel. Inside were the angel wings, although they had changed a little since the last time Luciana had seen them. Instead of being part of the doll, they were attached to a harness of thin leather straps made to go over a wearer's shoulders and around her waist.

"I've tested it myself as much as I can," Clara explained. "It's comfortable enough, and strong."

Luciana reached out to touch the harness. The leather straps were about an inch thick, but quite soft. "Won't the audience be able to see it?"

"It'll be hidden beneath your costume," Clara told her. "The wings will be under a layer of fabric so that when you turn, the audience won't see them."

"They won't really look like butterfly wings, will they?" Luciana asked. "Not with the feathers on them."

"Don't worry about that," Clara said. "They'll be so amazed by the overall spectacle it's unlikely they'll even notice. From a distance you'll be moving so quickly that they'll shimmer – the audience won't even see what they're made of. Now, when the time is right, you'll have to part the fabric of your dress with your hands –" here she made a flicking motion with her wrists – "so that the hook can find the loop. You'll have to time it exactly right and rehearse so that the motion blends in with the rest of your movements."

Luciana felt sick as the true enormity of her task hit her. It was down to her to make this believable. If she slipped up at any point, even just once, the game would be up and the trick ruined completely.

"Well," she said, a little shakily. "I'd better get that on so that we can start practising, hadn't I?"

"There's something else we need to show you," said Clara.

She pulled out two more strips of leather – shorter ones this time with ties on each end – and slipped them on to each wrist. Merritt stepped forward to pull the ties closed so that Clara wore them like bracelets. Running around the middle of each leather cuff was a very thin strip of dull silver-white metal. Clara held out both wrists so that Luciana and Charley could see them. Then she flicked her fingers and showed them the matches that had been concealed in her palms. A shiver ran down Luciana's spine, because she had just remembered the final aspect of the trick and she knew what was about to happen.

Merritt walked to the edge of the stage and picked up a bucket that had been hidden behind the curtains. When the magician returned, Luciana saw that it was full of dry sand.

Clara stepped back, then lifted her arms up and out in a swift, expansive flourish, crossing them in front of her as she brought them down again. There was the swift rasping sound of a match being struck, and then a sudden fizzing noise and Clara's wrists burst into a fierce blue-white flame. Luciana jumped and took a step back in fright, grabbing hold of Charley's hand. The flame silhouetted Clara in its glare, and the strange fire grew so bright that Luciana couldn't look at it without squinting. The light flared around Clara's wrists, turning her incandescent in its cold white glow for a handful of seconds. Then they snapped out of existence as swiftly as they had appeared. All that was left was a strange chemical smell and a last plume of thick grey smoke vanishing up into the dark cavern of the theatre's roof.

"What is it?" Luciana asked, once she found her voice again, the after-image of the fire still burning in her retina. She let go of Charley. "It's such a strange flame."

"It's magnesium," Clara said, as Merritt loosened the bracelets. "A peculiar metal that photographers use for their pictures because the light it creates is so great. It's the final distraction that completes the trick."

Merritt held up the two leather straps. They were still smoking.

"Let me see," Luciana said, trying to be bold. She took one of the bracelets between her fingers. The metal strip that had run around it was now curled and burned, and as she looked at it closely it flaked into ash and drifted away.

"It looks like burnt ribbon," Luciana said.

"Lucky for us, it's one of the ways they manufacture it," Clara said. "It's thin and narrow enough to conceal at a distance."

Luciana swallowed. "What would happen if one of those bits of burning ribbon were to fall on my skin?" she asked.

"It burns very hot," Clara admitted. "Very hot indeed. But the leather is thick enough to protect you, and the burn isn't long enough for the flame to catch it."

Luciana nodded at the sand. "That was in case you needed to put the fire out quickly wasn't it? Why sand, not water?"

"Because throwing water on burning magnesium would cause an explosion," Clara said calmly. "As I said … it's a very strange metal."

Charley's face was masked with worry. "But what if a

spark fell on to her costume?"

The thought made Luciana feel sick. Fear prickled along her skin. Though she tried not to, all she could think of was her nightmare. That terrible image of a figure trapped by huge orange flames, a wall of fire so fierce that there was no hope of escape. She felt Charley's hand on her shoulder, squeezing gently, and tried to tell herself that it was just a dream, that nothing like that could ever happen in real life. Except that only a day or so before, Clara had told her about theatres catching fire, and up there above their heads was Charley's lone stub of candle, waiting to be lit on the wooden rafter that helped to hold this whole place up.

"We won't lie," Carla said seriously, her words cutting into Luciana's worries. "It is dangerous."

Luciana still stared at the leather cuffs. "It didn't burn for long, did it?" she asked.

"Four seconds," Clara told her. "We've timed it precisely. Here's what will happen: You dance on to the stage. You hook yourself on to the line. Charley begins to lift you up even as the wings are opening. You will rise. The magnesium burns. The flames will die and at the exact moment that they do, every light in the auditorium will go out, just for a second. When the lights come back on again, you will have vanished. Charley will haul you up on to the bridge and wrap you both in a black blanket. You'll stay there until the final curtain comes down."

"But Luciana is so afraid of fire," Charley said. "She always has been, ever since she was little. It's the only thing she is afraid of."

Merritt looked at her with serious eyes. For a moment Luciana thought the magician was actually going to speak, but the moment past and he just tightened his jaw instead, frowning.

"It's not fair," Charley went on. "It's not fair to make her do that when—"

"It's all right," Luciana interrupted, proud that her voice stayed steady even though her stomach was churning. "I'll do it."

"You really think you can?" Clara asked.

Luciana handed back the leather bracelet with a shrug and a watery smile. "Yes. I can. I will."

Merritt stepped forward and put his fingers under Luciana's chin, tipping her face up so that he could look into her eyes. He looked deadly serious for a moment. Then he smiled. It was just a small smile, and a sad one, Luciana thought. It was far more Adeline than Adolphus.

"The show must go on," Luciana said, quietly. "Isn't that right?"

Chapter Twenty-nine

Luciana and Charley practised in the harness and with the magnesium for the rest of the afternoon and into the following day. The first time she lit the bracelets, Luciana was so fearful she thought she might faint clean away. Charley stayed by her side the whole time as they did that part of the trick over and over again. Luciana was determined not to let her fear win, however hard her heart beat every time the matches struck. After all, her grandmother had been right about at least one thing. Luciana had beaten her fear of fire once, and whatever had brought it back, she knew she could beat it again. They worked so hard that by the time Merritt and Clara began to get ready for their own evening performance, both Luciana and Charley were in sore need of a rest.

"Why don't we go for a walk?" Charley suggested, as he and Luciana headed backstage. "I don't know about you, but I could do with some fresh air."

They went down to the river, the noise of the city evening bubbling all around them. When they reached the Thames the tide was in, the inky water lapping high against her greasy banks. The river curved away in both directions, wide and deep, oily and dark, festooned by the myriad lights that lit buildings on both sides of the water. They reflected on the waves, watery sparks of yellow and white, rippling like fleeting magic. The river smelled of filth and salt, but she looked beautiful, enchanted.

Charley sighed.

"What is it?" Luciana asked.

"I've been thinking about what you said about our futures and about belonging. I'm trying to imagine going back to the attic room in Midford now. And actually, I ... can't."

She was surprised. "But you've been trying to go back home since we got here."

"I know. What about you? Can you imagine it?"

Luciana thought back. It was only a few days since she'd last woken in her own bedroom, and yet it seemed so much longer. She tried to think of exactly what she had done with her days before coming to London, and couldn't remember a single significant thing.

"No," she said. "I can't either."

Charley nodded, staring down at the water. "We'll have to go back though. Won't we? Or … *you* will, anyway."

A cold knot formed itself in Luciana's heart. "What do you mean?"

"Sitting up there in the rafters, I've had a lot of time to think," he said. "When this is over, you'll go back and look after that big old house. But I need to get a job. And I think I'd rather do that here than in Midford."

"You're going to stay in London?"

Charley shrugged. "I know people now – I'm friendly with Ben, and there's Timothy Fervent. Clara and Adeline, even. They've all got lives here. Maybe I could make one too. What have I got back in Midford except a bedroom I share with my mother and a job cutting grass for the vicar?"

Luciana stared down at the water and felt herself sinking like a stone, although it wasn't the Thames that was swallowing her up, but the thought of her own future. What would she do in that big old house for all those endless days except wait until someone wanted to marry her? Then the house would become his, his name would become hers, and she would have nothing of herself left. She wouldn't even have Charley. She supposed that this was what her grandmother had meant about different paths.

She couldn't bear to think about it, so she stood up. "Come on," she said. "Let's go and get some dinner. By the time we've eaten, the performance will be over. I want to rehearse some more before we go to bed."

*

They got back to the theatre shortly after 10 p.m. The noise of angry voices hit them even before Ben opened the stage door.

"What is it?" Charley asked. "What's going on?"

"It's Mister Carl Thursby," Ben whispered, his voice shaking. "He's in a mighty temper. He's in Mister Merritt's dressing room, yelling blue murder, so he is."

Luciana grabbed Charley's arm. "He must have seen one of our playbills!"

"So what if he has?" Charley asked. "What can he complain about? That he's not the only magician in town?"

"If it's not that, then … what?"

The answer occurred to both of them at the same time. Had Thursby discovered Merritt's true identity?

"Come on." Charley led the way down the corridor towards Merritt's room. As they got closer, snatches of shouted words made their way from behind the closed door.

"…a disgrace! It will not be borne! You pledged to uphold the agreement and now…"

They reached the dressing-room door. Charley raised a hand to knock but Luciana stayed his arm.

"…you will not even speak to defend yourself, sir!" Thursby finished.

Luciana opened the door. Inside was a tableau: Thursby, red with anger, faced an equally angry-looking Adolphus Merritt. Clara stood by, still in her stage costume and behind Thursby … stood Philpot Danvers. Luciana looked around each of them in turn before her gaze fell on Danvers.

"So it is true," she said. "You are nothing more than a spy. My grandfather didn't give you that puzzle box at all, did he? You stole it because you thought it held the Golden Butterfly."

Danvers had the good grace to look away.

"Well, well," sneered Thursby. "The prodigy who imagines she has a right to step on to the stage."

"We've met before," Luciana reminded him. "You ransacked my house on the day of my grandfather's funeral."

Thursby ignored her words, turning back to Merritt instead. "You have violated the trust of the Grand Society, sir, by allowing an unlicensed child to play at being an assistant. You have broken the most sacred of our laws and you will pay dearly for it."

"What is it you're really angry about?" Luciana asked. "That another Cattaneo is about to make a fool of you?"

Thursby spun back towards her again, his rage almost apoplectic. "You? Make a fool of *me*? Your grandfather was nothing but a charlatan, a half-rate trickster who would have done well to stick to touring with a grubby little circus on the Continent."

"And yet you spent so many years searching for the Golden Butterfly, and in the end the only way you could get it is by stealing from a child. What sort of charlatan trickster does that make *you*, Mr Thursby?"

Thursby curled his lip back against his teeth. "You are nothing. You are not worthy of the breath I have already expended in acknowledging your existence. You will never step on to this stage again. Phipps has already been warned that if you do, he will be blacklisted from hosting any magician in this theatre, ever. As for you," he said, turning back to Adolphus Merritt, "beyond these sins already enunciated, I have reason to believe that you are using a trick of dubious origin, one that seeks to mimic my own Golden Butterfly. You will show me its workings immediately. Only then will I, as the Grand Master of the Society, decide whether or not you can

222

proceed with your advertised performance."

"You have no right to demand that," Clara said, angry. "There is nothing in the Grand Society's Charter that says any magician must show you the workings of their illusions."

"Silence, girl!" hissed Thursby. "Who are you to speak against me? And what would you know of the Charter anyway? I'd be astonished if you can even read your own *name*."

"You still don't know how it works, do you?" Charley asked. "The Golden Butterfly. You still can't work out how to use it."

"This is not so!" Thursby exclaimed. "It was I who designed it, you ignorant whelp, it is my greatest creation, and mine alone."

"You are a liar," said Luciana. "More than that, you are a poor magician. And by next Tuesday night everyone will know it."

Thursby forgot himself in his rage. He raised his hand to strike Luciana across the mouth, but before he could a figure in black blocked his way.

"Strike a grieving widow and her granddaughter would you, Carl Thursby?" said Isabella Cattaneo. "Now, what *would* the papers say about that?"

Chapter Thirty

"Get out," said Luciana's grandmother to Thursby. "Now, this instant. I will deal with this."

Thursby stepped back, straightening his coat. "See that—"

"GET OUT," bellowed Mrs Cattaneo.

The two men left in silence. As Philpot Danvers passed her, Luciana's grandmother thrust a velvet purse against his chest.

"Repayment, as promised," she said. "With extra for letting me know the whereabouts of my granddaughter. Take it."

Danvers clasped his hand around the pouch and opened his mouth but Isabella waved one pale, imperious hand.

"Wait," Luciana said, before he could turn tail and leave. "The puzzle box."

Danvers flushed red. "I must go."

"You could never work out how to open it, because the puzzle was never meant for you, was it?" Luciana said. "My grandfather knew you had the box, but he also knew he'd never get it back alone. So he hid a second puzzle box in the Peacock Theatre, one that had your name and address in it. He hoped that one day, someone – *I* – would get back what you had stolen from him. You should be ashamed, Mr Danvers. Completely ashamed."

Danvers clearly had nothing to say to that. He turned and left. Silence reigned inside the room as the two men's footsteps echoed towards the stage door and then were cut off by its abrupt slam. A few minutes later Ben appeared in the doorway, his eyes large with fright.

"All the doors are locked? The theatre is empty save us?" Mrs Cattaneo asked him. When the boy nodded, she held out a copper penny. "Good. Now leave us. And if I catch you eavesdropping…"

Ben fled.

"Charley," she said next. "Stand in the open doorway. I want you to hear this but I also want you to make sure we are not disturbed. Speak if anyone enters the corridor."

Charley did as he was told.

"Grandmother—"

"Don't," Mrs Cattaneo cut Luciana off. "You," she said, pointing at Adolphus Merritt. "You are the one I want to speak to first. Take it off."

They stared at each other for a moment. Then the magician reached up and pulled at the nose that was his greatest illusion. A few moments later, Adeline Morrell stood before them.

Isabella didn't even blink. Instead she took a roll of paper from her pocket. In one deft movement she shook it out to reveal the playbill for Luciana's performance. She held it up.

"*This?*" she asked in an icy voice. "This is how you choose to repay everything that I have done for you?"

"Luciana came to us, Isabella," said Adeline. "*She* found *me.*"

"You should have turned her away. You should have sent her back to me."

"I tried, but it was too late," Adeline said. "She already knew, the moment she saw me, even if it took her time to realize it."

Luciana's grandmother tossed the paper to the floor in disgust. "So you put her on the stage?"

"She wanted to be there."

"How dare you? How *dare* you? And to use Marko's

name! When you *knew* Thursby would never let her perform anyway! Why?"

Adeline looked at her in silence, as if waiting for her to realize something. The older woman grew pale.

"No," Isabella said shortly, as if comprehending something for the first time. "You thought – what? That I would see the light and give you what you need to make this work? Absolutely not. *No.*"

"This is not how it has to end, Isabella. You know that."

Mrs Cattaneo turned away and for an alarmed moment Luciana thought she was going to faint.

"Grandmother," she said, reaching out a hand.

Her grandmother grasped it and pulled Luciana to her before turning to look at Adeline again.

"You wanted to force my hand," she said. "I thought it was Danvers who sent me the playbill, but it wasn't, was it? It was you. You knew I would come to retrieve Luciana, you knew I'd have to confront you – and what? You were relying on your powers of persuasion to wear me down?"

Adeline shook her head. "I just wanted you to see what Luciana can be if given the chance."

Mrs Cattaneo gave a hard, strangled laugh. "What? A plaything to be dressed up and painted like any other magician's assistant ... like her *mother*?"

Adeline flinched at that, and that single, tiny movement

unsealed a locked box at the back of Luciana's mind.

"That's not fair, and you know it," Morrell said, though her voice seemed distant.

"What then?" Mrs Cattaneo demanded. "What?"

Adeline said nothing. Instead she turned and opened a drawer in the desk behind her, pulling out a pack of cards. She threw the deck to Luciana, who caught it in one hand and then shook off her grandmother's hold to open it. It had been a few days since she'd had time to play with the cards. Having them back in her hands felt natural. Luciana started to shuffle and turn them as her grandmother watched.

"She's a magician, Isabella," said Adeline. "She's a *magician*."

Luciana continued to move the cards between her hands, casting trick after trick without pausing to look up. Focusing on the cards stopped her thinking about what had unlocked in her head, that little door that led to a huge room full of things she could not bear to look straight at. If she did, Luciana was afraid that she would begin to spin apart, that all the certainties of her life would scatter in opposite directions, a thousand tiny pieces that she would never be able to put back together. But even concentrating on the cards couldn't stop the world from turning around her, or stop her hearing the conversation going on over her head.

"You wanted her to have a better life," said her grandmother.

"She's *had* a better life," said Adeline. "She's had the best life she could ever have had with you and Marko. I could never have given her what you did, not after what happened. We both would have ended up on the streets if not for the two of you."

"Stop," Luciana heard herself say. "*Stop.*"

She looked up to find Adeline and her grandmother looking at her with sad, anxious faces. It was Adeline's that she studied though, trying to make sense of the connections her mind was beginning to make.

"You," she began, but her voice gave out and she had to start again. "Are … are you my mother?"

There was a moment of silence. For a second Luciana thought the world would continue as it always had. That Adeline would laugh, and her grandmother would laugh too, and then Luciana would be able to laugh as well, all at the sheer absurdity of such a suggestion. Except part of her knew that it wasn't absurd at all, because maybe, just maybe, it wasn't the first time Luciana had asked herself that question. And when the magician did use her voice, it was not to laugh.

"Yes," said Adeline Morrell, quietly but clearly. "Yes, Luciana. I am."

Luciana's eyes filled with tears. She looked down at the cards she held, and felt as if she were looking at a stranger's hands. Then she looked at Isabella Cattaneo, whose fire had been dampened by a look of weary defeat.

"So … then … you are not my grandmother," Luciana said. "And the Magnificent Marko wasn't my grandfather. Was he?"

There was another moment of silence.

"No," said Isabella Cattaneo in a faint voice. "Though we always loved you as if we were."

Luciana wasn't sure how much more she could take, but there was one thing she needed to know.

She looked at Adeline again. "Who is my father?"

Adeline looked away, though only briefly. When she looked back, there was a shadow in her eyes. "Anthony," she said. "Anthony Morrell. My husband, God rest his beautiful soul."

At these words another connection clicked into place.

"He died in a fire, didn't he?" Luciana asked, feeling as if she were one of Adeline's clockwork toys, unfurling mechanically as everything opened and snapped together in her mind, *click-click-click-click-click.* "Is that why I am so afraid of fire and why I have such terrible dreams? Was I there? Did I… Did I *see* it?"

This time it was Adeline's eyes that filled with tears, and

she did not blink when they ran down her face. "Surely –
but no… Surely, surely you don't remember that?"

"I do," Luciana said. "I always have. But until now
I never realized it was a memory. I thought… I thought it
was just a horrible nightmare. That's what my grandfather
– what Marko and Isabella always told me. But it was real,
wasn't it? It was all *real.*"

Adeline wiped away her tears with one hand and took
a deep breath. "You were so little. We always took you to
the theatre with us. When we rehearsed, we put you in a
basket in the corner, and every night when we performed
you would fall asleep in the wings. We'd check on you every
time we came off stage, and you were always so good. Most
of the time you slept right through." Adeline frowned and
shut her eyes. "The fire started one afternoon, while we were
rehearsing. Your father was under the trapdoor beneath the
stage, waiting for my cue, and suddenly the place was alight.
The flames were in the rafters before we even realized what
was happening. I couldn't save you both. I tried, but I was
too late. I only had time to undo the trapdoor and then
run to pick you up from your basket as the flames began
to surround us. Anthony got out of the trapdoor but by
then we were separated by the fire. I hoped…" Adeline's
voice trembled. "I hoped that he'd be able to find another
way out while I ran for the stage door with you. But when

231

I got out on to the street, I couldn't find him, and it was too late. I'm so sorry that you remember it, Luciana. It haunts me and always will, but I thought – I hoped – that you would be too young."

"Was it Thursby?" Luciana asked. "Did he start the fire?"

Adeline looked away. "It was never proven. But he hated Anthony. He hated our show, because it was better than his."

"And then you just ... gave me away?"

Adeline shut her eyes with a frown, and more tears slipped down her cheeks. "I didn't want to. I kept you as long as I could. But no one would hire me with a baby. Not until Marko, and even then I had to keep you hidden so that the theatre managers didn't find out. I lied and said I had left you with relatives – no one knew that your father and I had no one but each other. You were still so good, but you were growing and anyway..." she trailed off.

"You wanted a better life for me," Luciana finished. Her voice sounded hollow, even to her own ears.

"Yes," Adeline whispered.

Luciana looked at Isabella. "Did you want me?" she asked. "Or did Marko have to persuade you?"

Isabella let out a shuddering breath and pulled Luciana back into her arms, holding her tightly. "Of course I wanted you. Children had never happened for us, but oh, how I wanted them. Then your grandfather showed me this dear little scrap of life and said you needed a home. He said we'd move to a new town and say that our daughter and her husband had died back in Italy and left us with their child to raise. And that was that."

Luciana pulled away from Isabella, trying to fathom the depth of everything she had learned. "Is that why I don't remember ever meeting Adeline when we came to Grandfather's shows? You kept me away from her. In case I remembered her."

Isabella Cattaneo smoothed her hands over Luciana's cheeks. "When I learned that Adeline used to take you to the Peacock and hide you in her closet, I said we shouldn't take you back there for years. Just in case you remembered. We all decided it would be for the best. It seemed to work."

Luciana pulled away again. She felt light-headed, as if her mind was spinning on an axis no longer attune with the world around her.

"So what now?" she asked. "I'm supposed to go back to Midford and forget that any of this happened?"

Isabella looked down at her. "Would that be such a bad life? You've seen what this one is like. So … precarious, so *dangerous*. Is this really where you would prefer to be?"

"Yes," said Luciana, simply. "It is."

Mrs Cattaneo paled a little. "You may think you're an

adult, Luciana, but you are not. Not yet. And until you are it is my duty to keep you from doing foolish things, and this is most definitely one. You will come with me now, please. It is late enough as it is and I have booked a room for us at the Savoy. Tomorrow we will return home. In a week or so all of this … will have faded away. Then we can talk again about all of it if you wish, but in a sensible manner."

Luciana looked at Adeline, who gave a faint smile.

"Go," said her mother. "It's for the best, Luciana. We'll meet again soon."

Chapter Thirty-one

The room at the Savoy was not big enough for all three of them.

"Charley can stay at the theatre another night and we'll collect him in the morning," Mrs Cattaneo said briskly, as they got into the hansom cab. "It'll give him time to think about what he's done."

"What do you mean?" Luciana asked. "He's done nothing. This was all me. I talked him into coming to London."

"If he had any true loyalty he would have disclosed where you were to me at the first opportunity," said Isabella.

Luciana watched the theatre recede as they pulled away.

"He was being loyal to me," she said quietly. "As only a true friend is."

They were silent for a few minutes. Luciana was still a tumult of emotion, trying to sort through everything that had happened. She had a mother – a real, living mother. Luciana didn't know what to think. Her mind was a mess of questions, her heart full of confused emotions.

Isabella reached out and grasped her hand. "I love you, Luciana. Everything I have done and will do is for you. You have to believe that. We were trying our best, all three of us. In the end, that's all anyone can do."

Luciana squeezed her fingers briefly and then pulled her hand away. After a moment Isabella leaned back.

"I can't bear the thought of you leaving me," she said, her strong voice wavering a little. "I have already lost Marko. Must I lose you too? Have you forgotten all the wonderful times we had in that house as you were growing up?"

"Of course I haven't," said Luciana, "and of course you will not lose me. But being here, in London – doing these things … *that's* who I am, isn't it? It's who I've always been, even when I was small. Persuading Charley to help me stage tricks in our hallway. Climbing trees even when you told me I shouldn't. Sneaking off to read books instead of sitting at the embroidery you had given me. Getting up in the middle of the night to lie in the orchard and look up at the stars. Solving puzzles. Learning *magic*."

Isabella looked away. "I always told Marko he shouldn't teach you such things. I always said it would lead nowhere good."

"He only ever encouraged what he saw there already," Luciana said. "I loved my life in Midford with you," she said quietly, trying to find the words to explain everything she felt. "I loved – love – you, and Marko, and I always will. I'll always be grateful for everything you gave me when you didn't have to. But I'm not the same person that I was last week. And I think … *this* is where I belong." Luciana sighed. "None of it matters anyway though, does it? I don't have a licence. I can't perform."

"Does that really upset you so much?" Isabella asked. "Were you really so keen to be on the stage?"

"It wasn't just about me," Luciana said. "If people saw the Golden Butterfly, everyone would love magic again. Adeline would get her illusion back and everyone would remember the Magnificent Marko. People should know who the greatest magician in the world really is. But now they will think it is Thursby. Or else he will mess up the trick completely and people will care about seeing great magic even less. Grandfather wouldn't want that, would he? He was so sad that the profession was fading away."

They arrived at the Savoy and were ushered up to their room. It wasn't until Isabella was tucking the blankets around her that Luciana realized how exhausted she was. By the time the familiar kiss landed on her forehead, she was already mostly asleep.

A quiet knock at the door woke her some hours later. She half opened her eyes. A rustle and a shadow passed the end of her bed as her grandmother went to the door and opened it, took something, and then shut the door again. Silence settled over the room once more, pulling Luciana back down into sleep.

*

The following morning they took another cab back to Weston's Theatre.

"You go in, dear," said Isabella. "I'll wait here. Oh – and give this to Adeline, would you? Tell her it's from me. With –" she hesitated for a moment – "with my blessing."

It was a slim white envelope, fastened shut with a blob of red wax that had her grandfather's seal pressed into it.

"What is it?" Luciana asked as she took it.

Isabella smiled a little. "Something else she gave up long ago."

Charley was waiting for her in Clara's dressing room. "They're already down on the stage," he told her. "They've been there for hours. They're trying to work out how to run the show without you."

Guilt poured over Luciana like cold water. "Poor Clara. Who will they get to be up in the rafters instead of you?"

Charley looked down at his feet and dug his hands into his pockets. "Actually, I think I might stay. I'll come back to Midford soon to see Mother and explain everything … but they really need me here. And it's a job, isn't it?"

Luciana thought her heart might break. "Yes, I suppose it is."

He looked at her, his eyes anxious. "Do you mind? If I do it even though you're not the one performing?"

"Of course I don't mind, you'll do a brilliant job," Luciana said, determined not to make him feel bad. "And Clara will feel safer knowing you're up there for her." They stood there together, awkward, until she said, "I want to say goodbye to them both."

Down on the stage, they found Clara on the suspended wire. She was just a few feet off the boards, but she was shaking like a leaf. Ben was on the bridge and let her down again.

"Oh, Clara," Luciana said. "I'm so sorry. Why don't you just take the trick out of the performance?"

"We can't do that," said Clara. "It's bad enough that we've advertised it as the granddaughter of the Magnificent

Marko and it won't be. If we don't do the Golden Butterfly, there'll be hell to pay. I'll be all right."

Luciana turned to Adeline, hidden behind Adolphus Merritt's face. Those blue eyes looked down at her, anxious now, and Luciana searched them, trying to find more memories to fit them to. Even though it was true, it hadn't yet sunk in that this person was her mother, not really. She wasn't sure it ever would.

"Will you come to visit?" she asked. "Come to Midford one day. Please. I don't want to—"

Adeline reached out and pulled her into a hug. It was only when they parted that Luciana remembered the envelope.

"Here," she said, passing it over. "From my grandmother, with her blessing, she said."

Merritt frowned and undid the seal. Inside was a folded document that had yellowed a little with age. The magician unfolded it and gave a tiny exhalation of shock.

"What?" Luciana asked. "What is it?"

Merritt held it out. Luciana took the piece of paper and looked at the elaborate text that unfurled across the narrow sheet. It was Luciana's birth certificate. In the space for the father's name it read:

Anthony Luca Morrell

And then beside 'Profession, if applicable' it said:

Magician, licensed

Beside the space for 'Mother's Name' it said:

Adeline Annabelle Morrell

On the line for profession it read:

Magician's Assistant, registered

Below that, beside the space for 'Child's Name', was written:

Luciana Estella Morrell

Seeing her name written down like that, alongside her parents, made Luciana's eyes fill with tears. As much as she loved Isabella and Marko, here at last was her own family. Her own mother and father.

Adeline – because for that moment it was completely Adeline, despite the mask – cupped her hands around Luciana's face, her own eyes very bright.

"I won't let you go again, Luciana," she whispered. "I promise. And I will tell you all about your wonderful father. He loved you, little one. So very much."

They hugged, hard, and Luciana never wanted to let go.

"Don't cry," said Charley, taking the old document from Adeline's hand. "Ana, don't cry. Don't you realize what this means? This means you can perform. Doesn't it? Don't you remember? Mr Hibberd told us, didn't he? Women could only be registered as assistants, but that they were lucky, because—"

"—because their daughters would be automatically registered!" Luciana exclaimed, pulling away enough to look up at Adeline's face. "Is that true?"

"Yes!" exclaimed Clara. "Yes, it *is* true! I suppose that's what your grandmother meant by sending this with her blessing. With this as proof of who you are, he can't stop you performing! You're a licensed magician's assistant, Luciana. You always have been."

Luciana ran from the stage. She ran all the way to the stage door and out on to the street, but the cab – and Isabella Cattaneo – had gone.

Chapter Thirty-two

Luciana, Charley and Merritt rehearsed over and over, every hour that they had left. Mr Phipps, who had been terrified by Thursby's threats, was won over by the proof of Luciana's birth certificate.

"You will take this to Thursby?" Clara asked him.

"I will," Phipps promised.

"Do not, under any circumstances, allow him to keep it," Luciana warned.

"Oh, don't you worry, I am not fool enough for that, Miss Cattaneo – or should I now call you Miss Morrell?"

"I am still Miss Cattaneo," she said. "For now, anyway."

"Very good," said the theatre owner. "It seems that magic really does run in your blood, my dear. It's only a pity that your own mother can't be here to see you perform too. But anyway – granddaughter, adopted granddaughter – what does it matter, really?"

Luciana thought that to some it mattered a great deal, though she didn't say so. Part of her was sorry not to have seen Thursby's reaction, but a far larger part of her was relieved that all she needed to do was concentrate on getting the Golden Butterfly right. She was still having trouble seeing the line as she danced out on to the stage. At least though her nightmares had lessened. It was as if, now she understood the source of her fear of fire, she was able to deal with it better. Her hands were steadier as the magnesium flared, and she no longer had to shut her eyes tight against its glare.

They sent a complimentary ticket to Timothy Fervent in the hope that he would come to the show. They sent tickets back to Midford too, for Charley's mother Agnes and Mrs Cattaneo, but received no reply.

"You never know," Charley said. "They might surprise us."

Luciana tried not to be bothered by Isabella's silence. She had also tried to push the new discoveries she had made about her life aside to better concentrate on her performance, but it wasn't easy. It was made even harder when Ben appeared during their lunch break on Friday afternoon, red-faced and puffing hard.

"Yer've got to see this!" he said, holding out a roll of slightly torn paper. "I can't hardly believe it! They're all over town, so they are! Everywhere we've put a poster, 'e's put one too!"

Luciana took the paper and unrolled it to reveal a poster. It was bright yellow, and it read:

Carl Thursby, Grand Master of the Grand Society of Magicians, Invites All Right Minded Peoples to See the Treachery and Poor Practice of Adolphus Merritt and his Unqualified Assistants.

Watch this Simple Illusion Fail!

Laugh as Adolphus Merritt is Proved a Fool!

Then Attend a True Magician – The Greatest Magician in the World!

Beneath this was the performance date of the Golden Butterfly, along with this message:

(Two Penny Reduction for Every Man, Woman and Child Bringing a Ticket Stub from Weston's.)

Luciana felt sick.

"Why would he encourage everyone to come to our performance?" she asked. "Surely that's the opposite of what he wants?"

"He wants you to be heckled to death, is my guess," Ben said. "He's banking on a rowdy crowd."

245

Charley slipped his arm through Luciana's. "Forget it, Ana," he said. "It's just another of Thursby's horrible tactics. He wants you to be anxious."

"Oops," Ben said, looking worried. "I shouldn't have shown you, should I?"

"It's all right," Charley told him. "Luciana will be fine. She'll put Thursby in his place, just you see."

Ben beamed. "I bet you will an' all," he said to Luciana. "And I'll be there, cheering you on. So you know there'll be at least one friendly face in the crowd, don't you?"

"Thank you, Ben," Luciana said faintly.

"Yes, we knew about it," Clara admitted, when they confronted her about Thursby's challenge. "We expected it. It's not the first time he's pulled such a stunt."

"I wasn't expecting it!" Luciana exclaimed. "Why didn't you tell me?"

"We knew it would unsettle you," Clara said. "Look, the best thing – the *only* thing you can do is ignore it and just focus on the performance. Thursby's setting himself up to fail. He'll make a fool of himself without even trying."

"You don't know that," Luciana said with a quiver in her voice. "I still keep missing the line. If I hesitate, if I look for it in front of an entire audience, someone will spot what I'm looking for."

Clara gripped her by the shoulders and squeezed. "Trust

me," she said. "You are going to perform it the best you ever have, just when it matters the most. I have faith in you. So does Merritt."

Luciana tried to believe her. She really did.

*

On Saturday, Luciana woke so early that not even Ben was up. She crept out of Clara's dressing room with a lit candle and went down the darkened corridors to the auditorium. She stepped on to the stage and walked right to the edge, until it felt as if the dark void beyond might swallow her up. Luciana tried to imagine each seat lined with a different face.

She turned her back on that great darkness and walked back to the wings, putting down the candle. She began to dance, moving in and out of the light. She imagined herself being pulled by an invisible force. It was not she who would perform this trick, after all, but the great magician Adolphus Merritt. Everything would happen exactly as it should, because this was nothing less than magic.

Luciana opened her eyes. For the first time in all of her rehearsals, she saw the line and its hook with absolute clarity.

Chapter Thirty-three

The sound of the gathering audience was thunder over their heads. By the time the clock touched half past the hour of six, the theatre bar was so crammed that Ben reported a queue out into the street.

"They'll have to start letting people get to their seats early," said Ben, "or there'll be a right scramble when the doors open."

Timothy Fervent came to the dressing rooms to wish them all luck.

"Not that you need it," he said. "That crowd up there are as gentle as lambs."

The stamping and hollering Luciana could hear suggested the contrary, but she appreciated his efforts.

At seven they had only half an hour until showtime, and Clara shooed out everyone who didn't need to be there.

"You'll be right, lass," said Timothy Fervent, squeezing her hand. "You're as sharp as your grandpa, I can tell. He'd be proud of you. You're going to knock 'em all on their behinds."

Left alone in her dressing room, Luciana thought about Charley. He was already up on the bridge and had been for at least an hour. It was important there was no hint of preparation that might tip the audience off, so he would have to stay up there for the whole performance, even though he would only be needed for the final few moments of the final turn – the Golden Butterfly.

A little while later, Clara tapped on her door. "They've let the audience in," she said. "Will you come? There's something I think you should see."

Luciana followed Clara on to the stage. The noise beyond the curtain was huge. Clara pushed it aside, just a fraction. The auditorium was heaving. Rows and rows of people bellowed and called to each other. It was a scene of utter bedlam, and the noise was terrific. Luciana's fingers were numb with fear.

They're never going to settle, she thought, scared. *They're going to scream and shout and wail like this all the way through, but most of all when I step on to the stage.*

The auditorium door opened and a moment later

249

came a sudden hush. It washed through the audience, which quieted in an instant.

The figure that entered was Carl Thursby. He still wore his top hat and carried his silver cane. Behind him came Philpot Danvers. Then came another gentleman, then another, all dressed the same. They kept coming as Thursby kept walking, as if he were pulling an elaborate chain of rabbits from a hat

"It's the Grand Society," Clara whispered in her ear, as they reached the two empty rows of seats in front of the stage. "The *whole* Grand Society."

The silence persisted until Thursby reached his seat, right in the centre of the very first row. Then he turned to the audience. He removed his hat and bowed with an exaggerated flourish.

"Tonight, ladies and gentlemen," he announced loudly, "we will all witness a great undoing!"

His words acted like a signal to the temporarily tamed crowd. They bayed in delight, like hounds with the scent of a fox in their nostrils.

The blood drained from Luciana's face. She staggered backwards, but Clara held her tight.

"Don't think about them," Clara said into her ear. "They don't matter, not a whit. They're nothing but stuffed shirts and wasted breath. Look – that's what I wanted you to see! Up there!"

She pointed up to the balcony, to one of the boxes. Luciana looked and saw her grandmother. Isabella Cattaneo was glaring down at Carl Thursby with an expression of utter disdain. Beside her was Charley's mother, Agnes.

"She came," said Clara, hugging Luciana again. "Your grandmother's here to see you. That's all that matters, isn't it?"

"Yes," Luciana whispered, though she knew Clara would not hear her over the noise of the crowd. "Yes, that's all that matters."

She looked up into the rafters, hoping to catch a glimpse of Charley, but all she could see was darkness.

*

The audience did not calm down, not even once the curtain had lifted and the show had begun. Luciana tried to stay in Clara's dressing room, but in the end she found it worse to sit alone and imagine what was happening instead of seeing it for herself. As she made her way down the narrow dim corridor towards the stage, a figure dressed all in black rushed the other way, a large hat pulled down over its face.

"Hey," she said to the approaching figure. "You're not supposed to be here. No one's allowed backstage. Who—"

The figure didn't stop but instead barged its way past Luciana so hard that she was thrust against the wall.

"Hey!" she called after them. "Hey, stop!"

The figure did not pause, and there was no one else around to help. Afraid, Luciana ran towards the stage, convinced she would see flames billowing from the wings. But there was no sign of sabotage, or that anything at all was amiss – besides, that is, from the terrible sound of the crowd in the auditorium.

Mr Phipps stood in the dim light of the wings, wringing his hands.

"They're not here to be entertained," he said, agitated. "They are here for blood and I am afraid of what will happen if they do not get it! They may rip the theatre apart!"

"There was a man, did you see him?" Luciana asked. "He ran past me just now. I didn't know who he was."

"I saw no one," Mr Phipps moaned, "but I can hear them, right enough!"

Clara came off stage, the smile that had been plastered on her face since the show began failing the moment she was in the wings. Beads of sweat dotted her anxious brow. She faltered as she saw Luciana and tried to put the smile back into place.

"Oh, Luciana," she said. "You would do well to stay out of sight for now, dear."

"What's happening?" Luciana asked. "Is Merritt all right?"

"Oh," Clara said with a faint smile, "Merritt is always all right. You'll see, this next trick always wins over a difficult crowd. They always like the severed head."

But today it seemed not even the astonishing spectacle of Adolphus Merritt severing and then reattaching his own head was enough to quell the savage crowd. The booing just became louder.

"It's no good," Mr Phipps shouted to Clara over the din. "They're only here for the Golden Butterfly. You'll have to cut the rest of the show before they become complete lunatics!"

As if on cue, a chant started up from the auditorium. It began quietly, almost like a whisper, but grew and grew, louder and louder, the voices becoming rougher by the second.

Golden. Butter. Fly.
Golden. Butter. Fly.
Golden. Butter. FLY!
Golden Butter-FLY!
Golden Butter-FLY!
GOLDEN BUTTERFLY!
GOLDEN BUTTERFLY!
GOLDEN BUTTERFLY!

Clara peered around the curtain and then withdrew with a scowl on her face.

"It's Thursby," she said. "He's got them all chomping at the bit."

"You must go on," said Mr Phipps. "You must. I'm going to the box office. Someone will have to send for a constable!"

He bustled away. The chanting went on and on. Luciana took Clara's place at the curtain as Merritt stumbled off stage. The orchestra started up a new tune, a version of a song that was very popular in the music halls, but no one joined in. Luciana looked out to see Thursby, an ugly smile on his face. As she watched, he stood and turned to the audience. Then he spread his arms wide and gestured to the empty stage. The crowd erupted into raucous laughter.

"Phipps is right," Clara said. "We have to cut the rest of the show and go straight to the finale. Luciana – can you still do it?"

"Of course I can."

"Good girl. Then get ready – the costume and rig are over—"

Clara turned and pointed to a table that had been standing just behind a dressing screen to the right of the stage. But the screen was lying flat on the boards, as if someone had tipped it over.

They ran to the table. Luciana expected to find the harness bearing the mechanical wings gone, but it was still there. Yet what was left of it was almost worse than if it had been stolen.

"Oh no," whispered Luciana. "Oh *no.*"

The wings had been wrenched open, and the silk of their feathers had been ripped roughly from the frame, so that all that was left were the thin struts, the clockwork bones of their mechanism. Without them they looked flimsy and skeletal. Luciana wasn't even sure that the audience would be able to see what was left of the wings at all from where they sat.

"This is Thursby," Clara whispered. "This is his revenge."

Even behind the mask of Adolphus Merritt, Luciana could see that Adeline's face was devastated.

"We have to go on anyway," Luciana said, raising her voice over the crowd.

"We can't," Clara told her. "If we go out and perform like this, we'll be a laughing stock. Not only that, everyone in the audience will be able to see how the trick is done. It's over. We're finished."

Adeline turned away, covering her hidden face with her hands. Luciana looked around, trying to think of a way to save them. Her eyes caught on two small objects that had dropped to the floor as the vandal did his work. It was the leather bracelets bearing the magnesium.

"Wait," she said, an idea bursting into her mind, as bright as the metal's white-hot burn. "How much magnesium do you have?"

Clara spread her hands. "Why?"

Luciana grabbed the tattered wings. "Do you have enough to make these blaze?"

Merritt turned to stare at Luciana.

"The strips are thin enough to fit on to the outside of the frame and still allow it to close," Luciana said urgently. "The wings won't have feathers but they'll burn as brightly as a star. I think that'll be enough of a distraction, don't you?"

Merritt and Clara stared at her. "We can't do that!" Clara exclaimed. "We'd need to rehearse with it, test it, make sure that—"

"We don't have time," Luciana said. "We barely have enough time to set this up at all. Listen!"

The crowd had become even louder and were stamping their feet so hard that the entire theatre was shaking.

"It's too dangerous," Clara said, "and with your fear of fire—"

"I'm not afraid any more," Luciana said. "Or at least not enough to stop me. I'm angry. I'm more angry than

I have ever been before in my life. I am telling you, I can do this. *We* can do this. I won't let Thursby win. I will not let him destroy any more brilliant magicians or their magic. I won't be the one to burn. *Thursby* will. And I want it to be enough to *bury* him the way you had to bury my father; the way we buried the Magnificent Marko. So. How long will it take to set the magnesium?"

The magician shook her head. The crowd continued their racket.

"Come on!" Luciana cried. "What? Five minutes? Ten? It's now or never. If we don't get this right, you're going to lose everything anyway, Adeline!"

The magician's eyes flashed at the use of her real name. Clara gasped, but Luciana ignored it.

"Clara – you're going to have to buy us time," she said, already beginning to pull on the rest of the costume.

"Me?" Clara asked. "I can't do anything!"

"You can do plenty," Luciana said, passing the harness to Merritt. "Go out there and do every trick you can think of, all on your own. Then finish it with that disappearing number. Let's see what Carl Thursby thinks of that, shall we?"

"I can't!" Clara said again. "He'll take my licence!"

"He won't have to. If we don't do the Golden Butterfly by the end of the night we'll be finished anyway."

The voice was Adeline's own, cutting through the melee like a whip-crack. She and Clara looked at each other.

"She's right, Clara," said the magician. "You know she is. It's now or never. Let's show this snake what we're capable of, shall we? Come on, my girl. If this is to be our final performance, let's make it the best yet."

Chapter Thirty-four

Adeline and Luciana worked fast over the noise of poor Clara being jeered and heckled by the crowd. When at last she threw her final firecracker and the smoke obscured her trapdoor escape from the stage, they were ready. Adeline took Luciana's cheeks between her two palms and looked at her from the face of Adolphus Merritt.

"It will burn for five seconds. No more, no less. There is one strip affixed to each wing. You're sure about this?"

Luciana nodded. "Go!"

Adeline smiled, and then to Luciana's surprise, leaned forward and quickly kissed her forehead. In the next minute she had gone, vanishing to the shadows at the other side of the stage.

Luciana tried to still herself, listening for the signal to begin her dance. She wished she could talk to Charley, who would have no warning that the trick had changed until the magnesium ignited below him.

Clara appeared, pale and breathing hard, but there was nothing more for either of them to say. Luciana knew the moment Merritt had walked out on to the stage, because the jeers from the audience took on a new tone.

Charlatan!

Cheat!

Imposter!

For the first time, Luciana properly understood Clara's fear of Adeline's true nature being exposed. For one of these things was true, wasn't it?

Then, rising over the chanting, came the tune she had been learning to dance to for the past week. It sang to her above the riotous insanity of the crowd: sweet, familiar. Luciana turned to Clara and smiled. Then she began to dance.

The crowd paused a little in their heckling, but the sight of Luciana appearing from the wings was not enough to stop them wanting blood. Their shouts grew louder once again. Luciana ignored them all, pretending instead that she really was under a spell.

As she reached the centre of the stage, a sense of calm

settled over her, despite the tumult that bubbled from the heaving darkness. At that moment Luciana realized, for the first time since she arrived in London, that she really did know what she was doing. She felt it in her heart and in her bones. As strange a life as being on the stage could be, it was hers. It was home.

She reached the line and felt the hook connect with the loop as surely as if it were the old bolt sliding home on the orchard gate in Midford. Luciana spread her arms wide – the signal for Charley to start the winch. For a split second she wondered if he was there, but then she felt the hard pull of the line.

She began to lift from the stage. A sudden hush fell over the theatre. From the audience it must have looked as if Luciana had begun to float. Luciana opened her arms again, a slow, graceful gesture which ended with her flicking her hands against her costume to part it.

She felt the mechanism of the wings activate. The audience was now quiet enough that she could hear the faint *click-click-click* of them opening, and then the tiny *snap!* as the last arm locked into place. At the same time she flicked out both arms, striking the tips of the matches she had concealed in her palms against the outer struts.

The magnesium ignited. A great flare of blue-white light exploded behind her, so bright that Luciana could see the looks of utter astonishment on the faces of the audience as she continued to rise into the air. The heckling shouts became noises of amazement.

Luciana tried to keep her head dipped forward, but still she felt the blaze of the flames. The heat of the flames was breathtaking and for a split second the old terror threatened to engulf her. On the stage below she could see Adeline moving into position, ready to throw the firecracker that would signal to Ben to cut the lights. *Just a few more seconds,* she told herself desperately, *just a few more—*

Then Luciana's hair caught fire.

She smelled it, a different kind of acrid stench to the smoke of the magnesium. Panicked, she reached up, almost forgetting how many pairs of eyes were watching her every move. At the last second she turned the movement into a flourish of her arms and brushed the ember from her hair, flattening her hand against the burning strands just long enough to extinguish them. The nascent flames died under her fingers just as the magnesium gave its final brilliant flare. Below her, Adeline deployed the firecracker, an extra distraction for the audience. The lights snapped out and in that instant Charley turned the winch faster, yanking her up, so that by the time the lights came on again a mere second later, there was no trace of the Golden Butterfly. There was only Adolphus Merritt standing alone on stage, victorious.

The audience erupted, not in heckles but in cheers.

Luciana reached the top of the line. Charley grabbed her, hauling her up the last small distance so that she could reach for the rafter. She tried to grasp the rough wooden strut with both hands and almost howled in pain. The palm she had used to quench the flame in her hair was raw and burnt. Shocked, she almost let go, but Charley caught hold of her and held her tight.

Beneath them, the audience was still in uproar. Shouts of *More! More!* echoed around the auditorium. Charley kept one arm round her and pushed the loop back down to make the wings retract with the other. Then he pulled their black blanket over them both, concealing them from any inquisitive eyes that may look up from below.

They clung there together in silence as below them the show went on.

Chapter Thirty-five

It was another thirty minutes until the curtain finally came down, but to Luciana it felt like three hours. Adolphus Merritt and Clara delighted the crowd – who just an hour before had been baying for their blood – with many of the illusions they had refused to watch before the Golden Butterfly had been conjured before them. Luciana shivered beneath the blanket, her burnt hand throbbing. Charley rubbed at her arms, trying to soothe her.

The curtain coming down was their cue to finally descend from the rafters. The crowd were still stamping and roaring as their feet made it to the boards backstage. Clara appeared from the wings before Merritt. She saw them and bounced over as if she were walking on air.

"Quickly!" she said to Luciana. "You need to get the harness off for the curtain call!"

Adeline appeared, flush-faced and happy. Behind her the applause and chants of *More!* echoed through the theatre.

"You should see Thursby!" she laughed. "He looks as if he's ready to explode! The other magicians are all applauding – they loved it as much as anyone out there. There's no way he'll be able to better that on Tuesday and he knows it." The magician grabbed Luciana in a bear hug. "Oh, my dear, you were wonderful. You were *beyond* wonderful!" She held Luciana away from her and then frowned at her pale face. "What's the matter?"

"She needs a doctor," Charley said. "She's burned her hand."

"It's nothing," Luciana said, not wanting to spoil the moment. "Really, it was just a spark."

"Let me see." Adeline reached for her hand.

"Well, well, well, *what* have we here?"

The voice spoke from directly behind Adeline. She froze, staring at Luciana with her eyes wide.

Carl Thursby.

Adolphus Merritt spun around to find him standing there with a nasty smile on his face.

"So you do speak," he said. "I had assumed you were

merely an imbecile, but it seems that you are, in fact, an entirely different type of fool."

"You can't be here," said Clara. "No one is permitted backstage when—"

"Silence!" Thursby barked. "You," he said to Adeline, "disgust me. You have worked money out of honest folk using false pretences. Even for a woman, this deception is a rank one."

"Thursby—" Adeline began, but he cut her off.

"You dare to speak back to me?" he hissed. "As if *you* somehow have something to say worth hearing? I preferred you when you were silent."

"Oh, I wager you did, Thursby," Adeline spat. "That you could ever consider yourself a better of mine, that's the mystery. You who could not perform but half of what you saw accomplished tonight – by a *woman*. What would everyone out there say to that, eh?"

Behind them, the crowd were growing impatient once more. The foot-stamping and yelling had begun again. Thursby curled his lip.

"You think any one of those degenerates out there would believe that any of these illusions could have been devised by a woman any more than I can? You stole them, each and every one. It is the only explanation. And moreover –" he continued, as Adeline made as if to speak – "I offer you this choice. Retire from the stage tonight and hand over every mechanism you have appropriated to me, or be exposed and bear the consequences of your repulsive subterfuge. I'll give you a moment or so to make your decision." He walked away, going back to his seat.

Adeline and Clara looked at each other.

"No!" Luciana cried. "You can't do it. You can't even contemplate it! You can't let him win!"

At that moment, Mr Phipps appeared, as red-faced as ever. "What's the hold-up?" He asked. "Your public awaits you, sir! You must go to them at once!"

Adeline looked at Clara for another moment. Then she turned to Luciana. "Where is your deck of cards?"

"In my bag," Luciana said, confused.

"Get them."

"Wait a minute," said Mr Phipps, registering Adeline's voice beneath Merritt's make-up. "What—"

"Can you use them even with your bad hand?" Charley asked.

Luciana flexed her sore fingers. "I can try."

Adeline turned to Mr Phipps. "Sir," she said. "You and every audience member out there are about to witness a first for the stage, in this very theatre."

"Ahh," said Mr Phipps. "Will it make me money or turn me bankrupt?"

"Neither, Mr Phipps, though I wager it will make this place the talk of the town."

The theatre owner beamed. "Well then, I say have at it!"

"All right," said Adeline, turning to the others with a deep breath. "Once more then. Clara, Luciana – watch from the wings. You'll know when to follow my lead."

And with that, Adolphus Merritt walked back on to the stage, alone.

Chapter Thirty-six

The audience cheered as Merritt appeared again. The magician walked to the centre of the stage, right above where Thursby himself sat. Merritt held up his hands for silence and the cheers subsided. A murmur rippled around the audience instead as they realized that the silent magician was actually about to speak.

The figure on stage took a deep breath.

"Ladies and gentlemen," began Adeline Morrell in her clearest voice. "Please, I pray your attention for just a few moments more."

At the sound of her voice, an astonished hush fell over the audience.

"I believe I am right in saying that many people here

tonight have enjoyed the performance," Adeline went on. "However, there is something you don't know. I am not quite what I seem."

As she spoke, a murmur rose again.

"I solemnly swear that each and every trick you have seen tonight has been my doing. And yet Mr Carl Thursby – he is seated here, right in front of me – has decreed that this cannot be so. He has also decreed that I must hand over all of the secrets of my tricks to him, so that he might add them to his own repertoire instead."

Luciana was watching Thursby when Adeline said this. He spluttered and went to stand up to protest, but the magicians on either side of him held him back.

"So," the magician on stage continued, over the growing muttering of the audience, "I thought that the thing to do is break my silence and reveal my true self."

And with that, Adolphus Merritt reached up and pulled off his false nose to reveal the face of Adeline Morrell.

There was a moment of silence.

"You see," rang Adeline's voice into the audience. "The Grand Society of Magicians – Mr Thursby in particular – does not believe that women can perform magic. And yet all of you have witnessed not one but three women doing just that all evening. The first is myself, Adeline Morrell. The second was my assistant, Clara Smith. Here she is."

With that, Adeline waved her wand at a point on the stage. There was a bang and a shower of sparks. The audience gasped as they cleared to reveal Clara, who took a flourishing bow, right in Thursby's direction.

"The third was Luciana Cattaneo, adopted granddaughter of Marko Cattaneo – the Magnificent Marko, and … my daughter, of whom I am very proud. Ladies and gentlemen: the Golden Butterfly."

Adeline raised her hands, spreading them out towards where Luciana stood, thunderstruck at this introduction. Charley grasped her shoulder.

"Go on," he said in her ear. "And don't forget to show them that you can use the cards!" He gave her a gentle push and Luciana found herself walking out on to the stage.

Luciana fed the cards from hand to hand as she walked towards Adeline Morrell, who was watching her with a smile. Luciana played with the deck, thinking back to how she had seen the Magnificent Marko perform with them himself. She threw them in the air and collected them back together again with ease. She held up the ace of hearts to the audience, then showed them how she'd put it back into the pack before reaching over and producing it from Adeline's ear.

Adeline turned and with a large, looping circle of her

271

wrist, pointed her wand at Clara, who began to lift into the air, until, with another flick of the magician's wrist, she hovered about four feet from the ground, without a single trace of fear on her smiling face.

"Well, ladies and gentlemen," Adeline called loudly to the audience, "do you think that women can perform magic or not?"

There was a second of utter silence and then a loud whistle and a whooping cheer exploded from two seats up in the gods. Luciana looked up to see Timothy Fervent on his feet, grinning, waving and hollering. Then someone else stood up and started clapping, and Luciana realized that it was Isabella Cattaneo. Her grandmother stood on the balcony, applauding, with Charley's mother on her feet at her side.

Then another pair of hands joined the ovation, then another. The noise spread as more and more people stood up and cheered. In just a few moments the whole place was on its feet.

Carl Thursby stood too, but only to push his way out of his row. Philpot Danvers scurried after him as he stormed out of the auditorium. The rest of the Society members, though, were clapping along with the audience. One of them walked towards the stage and climbed on to it. His coat tails flapped a little in the breeze from backstage as he approached Adeline with a warm smile.

"Tobias Creases, at your service, madam," he said. "May I please address your audience?"

Adeline gestured to the audience. "Please do."

Mr Creases moved to the front of the stage and held up his hands for silence.

"Ladies and gentlemen," he said. "I am Tobias Creases, Deputy Master of the Grand Society of Magicians and I think I can say with some confidence that in the near future I may just be receiving a promotion. I believe that I can also say, on behalf of the Society, that we have seen an extraordinary level of talent here this evening. And, in recognition of this, the Grand Society will happily grant an exception in this case and admit each of you as full – women – members."

He concluded his speech with a beaming smile. The audience erupted in applause once again, and Mr Phipps, standing at one side of the stage, gave an ecstatic thumbs up. Adeline, though, looked at Luciana and Clara.

"What do you think?" she asked them both quietly, as the noise died down.

"An exception?" Clara repeated.

"In *this* case?" Luciana added.

Adeline smiled. "That's what I heard."

Clara shook her head. "No," she said.

"It wouldn't be right," agreed Luciana.

Adeline nodded. "All right. Luciana – why don't you tell them?"

Luciana took a deep breath and turned to the audience and Mr Creases.

"We appreciate the offer, but no thank you."

A whisper rushed through the crowd. The magicians in the front row looked at each other, perplexed. Tobias Creases looked shocked beyond belief.

"'No thank you'?" he repeated. "You – all of you – are saying ... *no*?"

"We can't be the only women magicians," said Adeline. "There will be others. There *should* be others. But you said we'd be the exception in your society. And that's not right. So unless you let any woman who wants to be a magician join – then thank you, but no thank you."

"Let any woman magician join?" Creases spluttered. "Don't be ridiculous. We'd be overrun with absurdity. They'd want to paint the dining room pink. They'd clutter up the place with lace and babies. It would be the end of magic as we know it."

"No," said Luciana. "It would be a change, not an end. Everything changes, but that does not mean that everything ends. Like a butterfly, coming out of its cocoon. It would

274

be a new age, that's all, a new age of magic. Perhaps it would even save the profession. After all, it hasn't been doing so well of late, has it?"

"Well said, my dear," said Adeline. "In fact, Mr Creases, I am not so sure we need you at all."

Creases' face had turned a livid shade of purple. "Why, of all the ungrateful—"

"Grateful? To you?" Clara said, her voice indignant. "Why on earth should we be *grateful*? Are you somehow under the impression that we exist because of something *you* did?"

Creases continued to cough and splutter. "You'll never make it work. No one will want to see a show comprised entirely of women!"

"Why not?" Adeline asked dryly. "They've watched plenty comprised only of men."

Chapter Thirty-seven

"But how will it work?" fretted Mr Phipps, his champagne glass quivering in one anxious hand. "I'll be bankrupt! If I let you stay on the stage unlicensed, the Society will blacklist me! I'll never get another act again."

They were all in Adeline's dressing room. Outside, Ben was attempting to control the stream of Stage Door Johnnies that were all desperate to meet the one and only Adeline Morrell. Well-wishers, ill-wishers, autograph-hunters, journalists – they all wanted to get in to see the woman magician in person and at close quarters. Ben, poor boy, had been told that no one should be allowed in. Charley had slipped out and found Timothy Fervent, bringing him back through the theatre and backstage to join the party.

"Oh, you'll have plenty of people coming along, don't you worry!" Fervent said. "It's the best show I've seen since the Magnificent Marko and that's no word of a lie."

"That is praise indeed," said Adeline with irony, tying off the bandage she had been fastening over Luciana's burn. It was, thankfully, not as bad as they had first supposed.

"Eh, it were a shocker though, seeing you rip that nose off your face," Fervent went on, still excited. "I'd seen you close up and had no idea!"

There was a knock at the door.

"I said no admittance!" Adeline called.

"I thought you might make an exception for me," called back a familiar voice, and the door was pushed open to reveal Isabella Cattaneo.

Luciana leaped up from her seat. "Grandmother!"

Isabella's face was stern, but her eyes were twinkling. "Champagne? How lovely."

There was a second of silence and then Adeline said, "Please come in. I shall get you a glass."

"Thank you for coming," Luciana said, wanting to hug her but unsure whether she should. "I didn't think you would."

Isabella cupped Luciana's face in both hands. "My darling girl, I would not have missed it for the world. Your grandfather, God rest his soul, would have been so proud."

Tears filled Luciana's eyes. She blinked them away. "Do you really think so?"

"Oh, I know so. He would have loved every second – but especially the Golden Butterfly and what happened at the end. You were all marvellous."

It wasn't until she let go of it that Luciana realized she'd been holding her breath. They sat down and Adeline, also smiling, handed Isabella champagne. Isabella nodded her thanks as she took it.

"You're hurt," said Isabella, seeing Luciana's bandage.

"It's nothing. I can't even feel it."

Isabella shook her head. "It's hard, isn't it?" she said. "A life on the stage."

Luciana grinned. "Worth it though."

"I'm sorry to interrupt," said Mr Phipps. "But I really am worried about this, you see. You are all, as Mrs Cattaneo put it, marvellous. But you can't fill my stage indefinitely, can you? And if I can no longer get magicians to play here, what am I to do? Magic is going to be the only thing anyone wants to see on the stage for a very long time now."

"It seems to me," said Isabella, "that Weston's could make quite a name for itself as the home of female magicians. As Luciana said – these three can't be the only ones."

"But how to find them?" Clara asked. "They'll either

have spent years hiding what they know or they won't be trained – they'll have the inclination but no skill."

"We should start a school," said Luciana. "We could train girls like me who want to be magicians."

"What a fantastic idea," Clara said. "We can start our own society."

"Yes," said Luciana, excitement growing. "It would be for anyone who wanted to learn how to create magic of their own one day, no matter who they were or where they came from!"

Adeline looked thoughtful. "It's a nice idea," she said. "And it would ensure you'd never have to worry about the Society again, Mr Phipps. But a place like that – we'd need space. Places for the students to stay, room to train in a safe environment. Could we use the theatre for that?"

Mr Phipps looked uncomfortable. "I like the idea too, but this place has to earn money. The rent alone would put me out of business in a month."

"It sounds to me," said Isabella Cattaneo, "as if you need a house for this school of yours. Somewhere with plenty of rooms. Somewhere that isn't really being used properly at the moment. Somewhere … like our house in Midford."

Luciana gasped and threw her arms round her grandmother's neck. "Oh! Would you let us? Really?"

Mrs Cattaneo laughed. "Oh, my dear. How could I visit your grandfather's grave with a clear conscience ever again if I did not? Besides," she added, looking up at Adeline as Luciana pulled back, "this is all the family I have. Perhaps it is time to get to know it better."

*

Later that evening, once the hubbub outside had died down, Luciana and Charley saw Isabella and Agnes to their hotel and then walked along the river back towards the theatre. The lights of London were in full force beneath a sky full of stars.

"Will you still stay in London?" Luciana asked.

Charley considered. "I don't know," he said. "It depends. I was thinking that you'd probably need a fulltime housekeeper for this school of yours."

"A housekeeper?" Luciana laughed. "You?"

He shrugged. "Well, maybe just a sort of housekeeper. One that climbs up into the rafters of theatres and operates winches from time to time."

They laughed together until Luciana sighed. "None of this would have been possible without you," she said. "You stuck by me every step of the way, even when it was difficult."

Charley smiled. "Well," he said. "Every good magician

needs a good assistant." He grabbed her arm, pointing up at the star-littered sky. "Look! A shooting star!"

Luciana looked up just in time to see the last streak of light as it vanished from view, lost to the vastness of the universe. She knew from her lessons that the star itself was long gone, and yet here was its light, still burning through the night sky. It made her think of Marko's words.

Everything changes, but that does not mean that everything ends.

Luciana smiled. Tonight was a new beginning, and she couldn't wait for the future to start.

Acknowledgements

As always, huge thanks to my wonderful agent
Ella Kahn at DKW and my editor at Stripes, Ruth
Bennett, for first seeing the potential in Luciana's story
and then shepherding me through the writing and editing
process. The beautiful cover is the genius work of
Pip Johnson, to whom I am very grateful. Thanks also to
everyone at Stripes who work so hard to polish, publicise
and market these books, particularly Charlie Morris,
Lauren Ace and Ella Whiddett. Last but never least,
thanks to my ever patient and forever supportive husband
Adam Newell. You are far more than I deserve.

Sharon Gosling's first middle-grade book, *The Diamond Thief*, won the Redbridge Children's Book Award in 2014. Her young-adult horror title, *Fir*, published by Stripes, was shortlisted for Lancashire Book of the Year 2017. She also writes books and articles about television and film, and has written, produced and directed audio dramas. Sharon lives in a small village near Carlisle, in Cumbria.

@SharonGosling